continued . . .

"An interesting and fun cozy mystery populated by a host of quirky and enjoyable characters."   —*Curling Up by the Fire*

"I absolutely couldn't put this book down . . . The mystery will definitely keep you guessing 'til the end, and the characters will have you coming back for more!"

—*A Prairie Girl Reads*

50% off Murder

"If you love to shop 'til you drop, watch out for Josie Belle's first entry in a new mystery series—because murder's no bargain."

—Leann Sweeney, author of
The Cat, the Vagabond and the Victim

"An engaging mystery full of humor, a layered plot and even a little romance."

—Amy Alessio, author of the Alana O'Neill Mysteries

"*50% off Murder* is a great deal: There's mystery, romance and humor wrapped up in one entertaining package. As a bonus, there's no extra charge for those laugh-out-loud moments. I look forward to many more adventures from Maggie and her friends . . . Meanwhile, bring on those money-saving tips!"

—Mary Jane Maffini, author of
the Charlotte Adams Mysteries

"A fun, well-plotted mystery with the added bonus of some money-saving tips."   —*The Mystery Reader*

"Best friends, bargain hunting and murder! This new cozy mystery series has great promise, and I'm looking forward to seeing what the bargain-hunting babes of St. Stanley will be up to next."   —*Novel Reflections*

Berkley Prime Crime titles by Josie Belle

50% OFF MURDER
A DEAL TO DIE FOR
BURIED IN BARGAINS
MARKED DOWN FOR MURDER

Marked Down for Murder

Josie Belle

BERKLEY PRIME CRIME, NEW YORK

56048531

THE BERKLEY PUBLISHING GROUP
Published by the Penguin Group
Penguin Group (USA) LLC
375 Hudson Street, New York, New York 10014

USA • Canada • UK • Ireland • Australia • New Zealand • India • South Africa • China

penguin.com

A Penguin Random House Company

MARKED DOWN FOR MURDER

A Berkley Prime Crime Book / published by arrangement with the author

Berkley Prime Crime Books are published by The Berkley Publishing Group.
BERKLEY® PRIME CRIME and the PRIME CRIME logo are trademarks of
Penguin Group (USA) LLC.

For information, address: The Berkley Publishing Group,
a division of Penguin Group (USA) LLC,
375 Hudson Street, New York, New York 10014.

ISBN: 978-0-425-27136-0

PUBLISHING HISTORY
Berkley Prime Crime mass-market edition / September 2014

PRINTED IN THE UNITED STATES OF AMERICA

10 9 8 7 6 5 4 3 2 1

Cover illustration by Mary Ann Lasher. Cover design by Sarah Oberrender.
Interior text design by Laura K. Corless.

This book is dedicated to three terrific book reviewers: Lesa Holstine, Dru Ann Love and Cathy Cole. You ladies have been tireless advocates for the traditional mystery genre, and my life has been enriched immeasurably by getting to know each of you. Thank you so much for all that you do. You're amazing!

Chapter 1

"More flowers?" Ginger Lancaster asked as she walked into My Sister's Closet, her best friend's second-hand store, on the heels of Henry Dawson, the local florist. Joanne Claramotta and Claire Freemont followed right behind her.

The four women belonged to a self-titled group called the Good Buy Girls. They were friends who were all about bargain-hunting and thrifting, and since Maggie had opened her shop, it had become the hub of their operation and their unofficial meeting place.

"Yep, she's got another one," Henry said. "Looks like someone's got quite the admirer."

For the past three days, Henry had delivered a single red rose to Maggie Gerber with a card that had one word written on it. Maggie took the rose from Henry and felt her face grow warm. She was embarrassed but also a bit giddy from the attention.

"Thank you so much," she said. She tried to offer him a tip, but he waved her away.

"You keep your money, Maggie," he said. "I've been paid more than enough."

Maggie gave him a chagrined look, and his wrinkled, old face split into a smile that showed off his dentures.

"Well, don't hold back," Joanne said. "What's the word of the day?"

Maggie put the red rose in a vase with two others and opened the small card. The word *You* was scrawled in blocky script in a black felt-tip pen. She knew that hand-writing. It belonged to her boyfriend, Sam Collins, who happened to be the police chief of their small Virginia town, St. Stanley. Of course, when she had questioned him the previous two days, he had denied all knowledge of any flowers or cards.

When put together in order, the cards read, *Maggie, Will You*.

"Squee!" Joanne let out a squeal. Her long brown ponytail swung back and forth as she bounced up and down on her feet.

"That is just the most romantic gesture ever," Claire sighed. She pushed her black, rectangular glasses up on her nose. "I wonder what will be on the next card."

"I don't know," Henry said. "But I'm betting I'll see you tomorrow, and every day right up until Valentine's Day."

Maggie and the others waved to him as he left the shop. Ginger turned back to face Maggie and rested her chin on her hand as she leaned on the counter and studied the cards.

"So, what do you think he's going to ask you?" Her teeth flashed white against her brown skin and her dark eyes gleamed with delight.

"I don't know," Maggie said. "I keep asking him, but he denies knowing anything about it."

Ginger's eyebrows rose. "Do you think it's someone else?"

"No," Maggie said. "I recognize the handwriting."

"Don't freak out on me," Claire said. "But do you think he's going to propose?"

"No!" Maggie said. "No, no, no."

"Well, don't beat around the bush," Ginger said. "Tell us how you feel."

"We've only been dating for two months, not even, a proposal would be . . ."

"Romantic?" Joanne sighed, and the others did, too.

"I was thinking *premature*," Maggie said. She frowned at them. "Besides, logically speaking, it doesn't work."

"What do you mean?" Ginger asked.

Maggie leaned over the cards, and a hank of her auburn hair fell in front of her face. She tucked it behind her ear as she tapped the counter with her index finger.

"There are three more days to Valentine's day," she said. "So if he did have a rose and a card delivered every day, then a proposal really wouldn't work because, *marry* and *me* would only be two more days."

"Unless he's planning something even more spectacular for the next two days," Joanne said. She started jumping up and down again, and Ginger put an arm around her.

"Settle down, girl," she said. "You are going to jiggle that baby right out."

Joanne instantly put her hands on her belly and her eyes grew wide. "You think so?"

"No," Ginger said as she gave her a half hug. "I'm just teasing."

"How long now?" Claire asked.

"I'm eight months, give or take a few days," Joanne said. "My obstetrician says it could be anytime if baby decides to come early."

"A baby," Maggie sighed. "It seems like ages since I've held a wee one."

"So, if this whole card and flower thing does turn out to be a proposal, and you and Sam do get married, will you have another baby?" Claire asked.

"I . . . uh . . . huh?" Maggie stammered. "I'm sorry, I think I just swallowed my tongue."

Ginger hooted with laughter. "You could, you know. You're only forty-one. Why, there are women having babies well into their fifties now."

"But then I'd be in my sixties by the time it went to college," Maggie said. "And given that I already have a daughter in college, I don't really want to do that again. The financial aid forms alone are a solid case for birth control."

"But you're a very young forty-one. I mean, how many people think your grandnephew, Josh, is your son?"

"A fair few," Maggie admitted.

Maggie watched her niece's three-year-old often, and while she loved him dearly, he was another reason she knew she was done bearing children. After an afternoon spent with her Josh-by-gosh, she was exhausted.

"See? You're still young enough," Joanne said. "Just think, our babies could play together. We could have mommy-and-me time together, too."

"Aw," Claire said. "That would be so cute. You could put them in matching outfits and have teddy bear picnics and tea parties. Adorable!"

Maggie frowned at Claire. "Don't you start. You're younger than me. You and Pete could get married and have kids, too, you know."

Claire shook her head. "No, that's not in the cards for me. I realized long ago that I was not mother material. I never even babysat when I was a teen, because the sound of a baby crying gives me hives. There's a reason I'm an adult services librarian and not a children's librarian, you know. My cat, Mr. Tumnus, is all the dependent I can handle, thank you very much."

"Is Pete okay with that?" Joanne asked. "I mean, doesn't he want to have a family of his own?"

"Thankfully, no," Claire said. "We had a long frank talk when we first started dating, and we both decided that parenting was not our calling, so it looks like it's all on Maggie and you—unless, of course, Ginger wants to try again for a girl."

"Lord-a-mercy, no," Ginger said. "Four boys are all I can handle. Besides, after Dante came along, I had them take out all of my plumbing since it had begun to collapse. So it's just Maggie then."

Maggie put a hand to her forehead as a sudden attack of wooziness hit her like a freight train. Did Sam want kids? She had no idea. They'd never discussed it. What if he wanted to be a dad? What if he wanted more than one? Oh, man, how had this topic of conversation never come up?

The bells on the front door jangled and Maggie glanced up, willing someone, anyone, to arrive and save her from this discussion.

The woman who arrived was not her first or even her last pick, but times being desperate, she decided not to quibble.

"Summer Phillips," Maggie cried. She came around the counter and greeted the woman who had been her lifelong nemesis with a wide, warm smile. "Come in. How are you, dear?"

Summer froze in mid-step. She looked at Maggie as if she was worried that she was ill with something that could be contagious or deadly or both.

"You look deranged," Summer said in her usual abrasive tone. She tossed her long, bottle-bleached hair over her shoulder and held up a well-manicured hand to ward Maggie off. "You're not going to hug me, are you?"

"No!" Maggie protested. Although she was grateful enough for the interruption that she might give her a half hug or an air kiss. The sour look on Summer's face checked that impulse.

"What's wrong with you?" Summer asked.

"Nothing," Maggie lied.

"She's panicking," Ginger whispered to Claire in a voice loud enough to be heard by everyone. Maggie heard them all giggle.

"I'm just being neighborly. What can I do for you, Summer?" Maggie asked.

"Nothing," Summer said. "Believe me, I don't want anything from you."

"Then why are you in my shop?" Maggie asked. "You have your own consignment store across the street. Why are you visiting mine?"

A woman nudged her way into the shop behind Summer. She had the same pretty face as Summer, with an upturned nose and prominent cheekbones, but she was obviously older, with very fine lines around her eyes and mouth. Her hair was cut in a black bob, and it swung about her face in graceful sweeps as she looked Maggie over, from head to toe.

"Mom, this is Maggie Gerber," Summer said. She stood aside and crossed her arms over her chest. "Now that you've met her, can we please go? This shop gives me the heebie-jeebies."

"Your mother?" Maggie asked. She blinked. It wasn't like she thought Summer had been spawned from a pinecone; still, she hadn't seen Summer's mother in ages.

Maggie glanced at the woman still scrutinizing her. Yes, she vaguely remembered Summer's mother, Blair Phillips, from their high school days, but she knew Blair had been married at least three times since then, and she had no idea what her surname was now.

Blair's lips pursed to the side in a scowl, and her eyes narrowed. Then she shook her head. "No, no, I refuse to believe it. There is absolutely no way that Sam Collins threw you over for this."

Chapter 2

"Excuse me?" Maggie asked. She frowned at the woman in front of her. "I'm pretty sure my boyfriend didn't throw over anyone, especially not her, for me."

"No one asked you," Blair said.

Maggie glanced back at her friends to see if this was for real. Judging by the matching looks of irritation on their faces—yep, this was real.

"I'm sorry, unless you're here to shop or to consign something for me to sell, you're going to need to leave . . . now." Maggie was pleased that her voice sounded so calm when on the inside she was boiling.

Blair glanced around the shop. Her nose crinkled in distaste. "No, I really don't see anything in here that would interest me. I don't do the shabby-chic thing that you've got going on."

The front door opened and in strode a gray-haired man wearing a plaid shirt and jeans with a scuffed pair of cowboy boots. His wide leather belt seemed to prop up the beer belly he was sporting, but his smile seemed genuine as he took in all of the ladies before him.

"Well, I might have known you two girls would be off shopping the first chance you got," he said. His voice had a light drawl to it, but Maggie couldn't tell if it was age or origin that flavored his speech.

"Oh, no, we're not shopping," Blair corrected him. "We're merely checking out the competition—and we're being very generous by calling it that, believe me."

Maggie supposed she should consider it a compliment that Summer and her mother found her and her shop wanting, but truly it felt like a slam—a well-delivered one, at that.

"Hi, I'm Mr. Blair," the man joked.

He extended his hand to Maggie. Maggie and the others just stared at him, and he sighed, as if realizing that his wife had made his joke not funny.

"I'm Bruce Cassidy, husband to Blair and stepfather to Summer," he said.

Good manners propelled Maggie forward, and she shook his hand. "Maggie Gerber. Nice to meet you."

The others followed her lead, while Blair and Summer frantically whispered behind their hands.

Maggie was pretty sure they were shredding her shop, her hair and the outfit she wore today. She glanced down, trying not to appear self-conscious. She was wearing her favorite jeans—no, not skinny jeans, but the cut and fit were flattering—with a snug blue sweater. Possibly they were finding fault with her navy Converse sneakers, but today was the day she sorted inventory in her stockroom, and a skirt and blouse combo really didn't cut it for the heavy lifting.

"We're done here, Bruce," Blair declared. She strode to the door in her tight skirt and calf-hugging boots topped by her puffy jacket. Summer fell into step behind her, and it was then that Maggie realized the two women were wearing the exact same outfit but in different colors. Blair favored dark jewel tones, while Summer was all about the pastel, shiny fabrics. Neither Blair nor Summer bothered to say good-bye when they left.

Bruce gave Maggie and the others a shrug as if this were normal operating procedure.

"We've only been married two years, but she still keeps me on my toes," Bruce said. He smiled, but no one returned it. He tightened his scarf around his neck. "Ten years away from southern California and I'm still not used to the cold. Well, nice meeting you, ladies."

He caught the door before it shut completely and pushed his way out onto the street behind Summer and her mother.

"Heaven help us, there are two of them," Ginger said. She stood gaping at the window as if she couldn't believe her eyes.

"I think I need to find a happy place," Maggie said. "A very happy place."

She closed her eyes and concentrated on the Presidents'

Day sales that would be coming up in a matter of days. Sure enough, thinking about all of the boots, coats, gloves and hats that were to be discounted on the big sale day helped pull her out of her spiral of outrage, hurt, horror and revulsion. Summer and her mother could not touch her in her happy sale place.

"Are you all right in there?" Ginger asked after a few minutes. When Maggie didn't answer, she asked, "You're not catatonic, are you?"

Maggie blinked her eyes open. "Just mentally perusing the Presidents' Day sales."

Claire, Joanne and Ginger all nodded in perfect under-standing. Oh, yes, there was nothing a bargain hunter loved quite so much as a holiday sale.

"I refuse to let Summer or her mother ruin one of the best shopping weekends of the winter for me," Maggie said. "I've been tracking the Sunday circulars, and the big stores are having mega sales. I'm pretty sure I can load up on items to stock the shop for next winter."

"And we'll help," Claire said. "I saw Stegner's is hav-ing a buy two get one free on shoes."

"Perfect," Maggie said. "And this time, I want to branch out to handbags."

"Now you are speaking my language!" Ginger cried. She was known for her weakness for purses.

"I was thinking I could do a display of handbags in the window," Maggie said. "Too bad Laura isn't here. She's so clever with window displays."

Laura Gerber, Maggie's only child, was away at col-lege in Pennsylvania. Since Maggie's husband, Charlie, had been killed when Laura was a toddler, it had been just the two of them for as long as Maggie could remember. She missed her daughter terribly, but she wanted Laura to pursue her own dreams, even if it meant Laura didn't settle back in St. Stanley. As Maggie's own mother had told her when Laura was born, the greatest gifts she could give her daughter were roots followed by wings.

"She could always do a phone consultation," Joanne said. "Tell her what you're thinking of doing, and she will tell you how wrong it is and then give you fabulous advice."

"Is that what happened with your window display at the deli?" Claire asked.

"Pretty much," Joanne said. She and her husband, Michael, owned and operated the local deli More than Meats. "Michael did not understand why I felt it was so important to decorate the windows of our deli. I think it was pregnancy brain. Ever since the tragedy there, well, I just feel the need to make it over."

Maggie and the others nodded. One of Joanne and Michael's employees had been murdered in the deli just before the holidays, and they knew Joanne had been struggling to put it behind her and focus on her baby's arrival.

"So, were you leaning toward blue or pink for the decorations?" Claire asked.

Michael and Joanne had opted not to find out the gender of their baby. It had been driving Claire bonkers ever since Joanne had told her, and she never missed an opportunity to try and determine if her friend was having a boy or a girl.

"Neither," Joanne said. "I was mostly just obsessed

with naked cupids and big shiny red hearts," she said. "I texted Laura with my brilliant idea, and she convinced me that lacy white doilies cut into the shape of hearts would be much more festive on a deli window."

"Yeah, I don't suppose anyone wants to order a big ole hunk of ham when they're looking at a cupid's butt," Ginger said with a snort.

Maggie bit her lip to keep from laughing. It almost worked, but a small chuckle escaped before she could stop it.

Claire did not laugh but was instead eyeing Joanne's belly as if she could see inside. Maggie could tell the gender issue of Baby Claramotta was making her batty.

"Has Michael been gaining weight?" Claire asked.

Joanne frowned at her. "Why do you ask?"

"Because I read an article that said when a husband gains a lot of weight during his wife's pregnancy, then it's a girl," Claire said.

"How do they figure?" Ginger asked. "I birthed four boys, and the way Roger ate, you'd think he was the pregnant one. The man had worse cravings than I did."

"He's the exception that proves the rule," Claire said. She turned back to Joanne. "So, any new love handles on the husband to report?"

Joanne frowned as if trying to think. "I don't know . . . maybe . . . but I mean, he's not huge or anything."

Claire scrutinized Joanne's belly. "Okay, well the other thing I read was that if you carry the baby low, it's a boy, and if you carry high, it's a girl."

Ginger looked at Maggie and rolled her eyes. "For a

woman who prides herself on research, she sure is busting out the old wives' tales."

"I don't know," Joanne said as she studied her belly. "From this angle, I feel like the baby is sitting right smack dab in the middle."

Claire shook her head. "This is driving me crazy. How could you not find out what it is? Don't you want to know? Aren't you curious?"

Joanne hugged her belly. "I just want healthy. That's all that matters."

"Yeah, but how am I supposed to know if I should be stocking up on blue or pink?" Claire asked. "Sports teams or ballerinas?"

"Yellow and green are lovely, too," Joanne said. She reached into her purse and pulled out her phone to check the time. "Oh, I have to go. Michael and I have a doctor's appointment."

"Will there be an ultrasound?" Claire asked as they headed toward the door. "Can I come? The doctor could just tell me. I swear I won't blab."

"No, you nut," Joanne laughed. "You can't find out the baby's gender before us. Besides, you know you'd never be able to keep it a secret."

"I would, too," Claire insisted. "I'd just call it Cletus the fetus."

"Then I'd think it was a boy," Joanne said. "Listen, Claire, I love you like a sister, but no, you may not come to the doctor with me."

She pushed open the door and waved to Ginger and Maggie as she left.

"Fine, but don't blame me when all that baby has to wear is yellow," Claire said. She, too, waved to Maggie and Ginger, and the door swung shut behind them.

"The suspense is killing the librarian in her," Ginger observed.

"No kidding," Maggie said. "I don't remember carrying Laura high."

"You didn't," Ginger said. "You looked like you swallowed a bowling ball and were cradling it in your pelvis. How often did you have to go to the bathroom?"

"Every fifteen minutes," Maggie said. "And your boys rode high. Remember? Dante's foot was lodged in your ribs for weeks."

Ginger rubbed her right side. "How could I forget?"

The door to the shop opened and Sam strode in carrying a take-out bag from Slice of Heaven, the local pizza joint. Maggie could smell Mrs. Bellini's signature sauce all the way across the room.

"Hello, ladies," he said. He stopped beside Maggie and planted a quick kiss on her lips before handing over the bag.

"A man who delivers lunch," Maggie said. "You really are pretty perfect, aren't you?"

Sam grinned, and it made Maggie dizzy. She did not think she would ever get used to Sam being hers, all hers, again.

"Hi, Sam," Ginger greeted him. She kissed his cheek and gestured to the vase on the counter with its three red roses. "Nice flowers."

"I have no idea what you're talking about," he said.

Then he blinked at her, as if that made him look more innocent.

"Uh-huh," Ginger said. "Well, here's a word to the wise: If you're romancing Maggie, you may want to go for the big, public gesture that will have people talking for weeks and will keep Summer's mother at bay."

Sam frowned. "Am I missing something?"

"Apparently, we all were. Blair and Bruce Cassidy, Summer's mom and stepfather, are here for a visit and decided to stop by my shop to check out the competition," Maggie said.

"And?" Sam asked.

"Blair found Maggie less than satisfactory," Ginger said.

"What? Why?" Sam asked.

"Oh, how did she put it?" Maggie asked Ginger as she put the food on the counter and opened the bag to let the delicious smell perfume the room.

"In her opinion, you're not worthy," Ginger said.

"Not worthy of what?" Sam asked. He looked outraged, a fact that made him even more attractive to Maggie.

"Quote, 'There is no way that Sam Collins threw you over for this,' end quote," Maggie said.

"'This' meaning?" Sam asked.

"Me," Maggie said. "I was lucky enough to be the recipient of Blair's scorn. Clearly, she thinks I am not worthy of you. It was a good time."

"That's . . . um . . . let me find the right word." Sam paused. He scratched his head and said, "Insane."

"No argument here," Ginger said. "But if I were you,

Sam, I would watch your back, front or any other part you value, if you get my drift."

"Eep!" Sam let out a girly, high squeak and with a look of mock horror crossed his arms over his middle, which made Maggie and Ginger both laugh.

"Don't worry," Maggie said. "I'll protect your virtue."

Sam gave her a wicked wink, which made Maggie's face get hot with embarrassment. Ginger glanced between them with a wide smile.

"How I never knew that you two were a couple back in the day, I cannot imagine. You really are perfect for each other."

"That's because someone let Summer Phillips mess with her head instead of asking me for the truth, thus causing our dramatic teenage breakup before we told anyone we were even together." Sam gave Maggie a dark look.

"I'm never going to live that down, am I?" Maggie asked.

Sam and Ginger exchanged a look and then simultaneously said, "No."

In high school, when Sam and Maggie had just been getting together as a couple, Summer had her boyfriend of the moment put on Sam's football jersey. Then she staged a half-naked, passionate encounter for Maggie to walk in on, which she did, causing Maggie to believe that Sam was cheating on her. It ruined Sam and Maggie's relationship. He left for college, and they didn't speak again for twenty-plus years.

"Just don't let your guard down around Summer or her

mother again," Ginger said as she pulled on her coat and headed to the door with a wave. "See ya, kids."

Maggie took the bag from the counter and led the way over to a sitting area in the corner of her shop. It sported a glass coffee table and several mismatched chairs, all of which were available for purchase. When she had opened her secondhand store, Maggie had decided that one way to update its look was to make everything in it for sale, causing her furniture to turn over as often as her clothes, which kept the store fresh.

Maggie and Sam sat down on the love seat that was currently in residence, and Maggie unloaded the bag. Salads, bread and two cardboard containers with individual servings of lasagna were unpacked, and suddenly Blair and Summer's visit seemed ridiculous. This was the magic of comfort food, and Mrs. Bellini made the best in town.

"So do you think I should be concerned about Summer and her mother popping in for a visit?" Maggie asked.

"Nah." Sam dropped a kiss on her head and then leaned back to look at her with affection. "We're rock solid. What harm could they possibly do to us?"

Chapter 3

It did not take long for Sam's optimistic outlook to take a sharp turn south.

"How many times have you been called to Summer's shop over the past three days?" Maggie asked. She and Sam were fixing dinner in her kitchen while Marshall Dillon roamed around the house.

Maggie was glad to have Sam and Marshall there. Things had been awfully quiet since Laura had gone back to college, an event which had been followed shortly after by Sandy, Jake and Josh—her niece, her niece's husband and their son—moving into their own house.

They lived around the corner from Maggie's now, and she had dibs on babysitting Josh, but still, her house felt like an empty shell with no squeals from the three-year-old to break the quiet. She hadn't stepped on a toy in weeks, and there were no cracker crumbs on the furniture. It just seemed wrong, and she didn't like it. Of course, Sam now spent most of his evenings with her, and a lot of his nights, too, so maybe it had all worked out for the best.

"Five times. First they swore there was a burglar breaking in; next they were sure Mrs. Shoemaker was shoplifting." He paused while Maggie sputtered.

"But that's outrageous!"

"Agreed," he said. "Then they were concerned that someone was hiding in the dressing room. It was a stray cat."

"Summer probably caught it and put it in there just so she could call you," Maggie said sourly.

"You're cute when you're jealous," he said.

"I am not jealous," Maggie corrected him. "Just appalled that your time is being wasted by those conniving idiots."

Sam opened the oven and used a pot holder to take out the pan of freshly baked corn bread. "I do feel like they have me on speed dial."

"Have you sent other officers over?" Maggie asked. She lifted the lid to her Crock-Pot and checked on the pulled pork. She had put in the leftovers from a roast they had made a few nights before and let it cook all day in her favorite sauce. It looked amazing.

"Yes, but Blair insists she will only talk to me. Honestly, it's embarrassing," he said. He sighed, then he turned to frown at Maggie. "Are you laughing at me?"

"No." She clamped her lips together to keep from chuckling out loud. A snort came out of her nose instead.

"You are!" he accused.

"I'm sorry," Maggie said. She gave in and laughed out loud. "It's just that it's all so crazy. Blair really thinks that if she keeps throwing Summer at you, you will eventually crack and give in."

"I suppose I would laugh, too," Sam said, "if it wasn't happening to me."

"Maybe you need to find a bigger fish for Blair to cast her net at," Maggie said.

"Like who?" Sam asked. "Seriously, I'll take anyone."

"I don't know," Maggie said. "St. Stanley is not exactly hip-deep in available males. Obviously, Tyler Fawkes has been kicked to the curb."

"I really thought after the Madison ball that he and Summer were a thing," Sam said.

"So did I," Maggie said. "But then Mama Blair showed up."

"Tyler's not good enough?" Sam asked.

"Apparently not," Maggie said.

"Well, I've had plenty of time to observe the wacky family dynamic that is Blair Cassidy and Summer Phillips," Sam said.

"What have you learned?" Maggie asked.

"Well, aside from the fact that Blair's been married five times and Summer four—that's nine husbands between them—I think that Blair genuinely cares for her daughter and wants her to be happy."

"Which she assumes would be with you," Maggie said.

Marshall Dillon strolled into the kitchen and sat in the

middle of the floor. He blinked at them and let loose a yowl that was most definitely a complaint.

Maggie glanced down at the feline and smiled. "I swear the M on his forehead is wrinkling into a frown."

"Yep, that's his hungry face," Sam said. He crouched down on the floor, and Marshall Dillon stood on his back legs and put his front paws on Sam's knee. Then they gently bumped foreheads. As always, Maggie found this male bonding ridiculously charming.

"Well, I told him he has tuna from me for eternity after saving my life a few months ago," Maggie said. She leaned over and scratched Marshall Dillon's chin just the way he liked it.

"From me, too," Sam said. "I really would deputize him for saving my girl. Heck, I'd make him my sole heir if I could."

Maggie smiled. "I think you just need to feed the poor boy before he expires."

Sam stood, scooping Marshall Dillon up with him. Together they filled the food dish Maggie kept at her house for the cat. Sam watched his boy for a moment until he was satisfied that Marshall Dillon was happy with his dinner. It occurred to Maggie that Sam would have made a really great father.

She shook her head. While she was curious about why Sam had never married or had a family, it felt as if it was too soon in their relationship to ask such a personal question. She was sure Sam would tell her in time.

She dished the pulled pork into a serving bowl while

Sam cut up the corn bread. Maggie took the salad she had made earlier in the day out of the refrigerator and together they set the small table in the kitchen.

Sam poured them each a glass of beer and Maggie took the seat across from his. They both dished their food, and when they were done, Sam held up his glass for a toast.

"To many more evenings just like this with you," he said.

"I'll drink to that," Maggie said.

She tapped his glass with hers. She knew what he meant. It seemed as if she had been single for a very long time. And then, her high school boyfriend Sam had strolled back into town and taken the job of sheriff.

Their high school breakup had been the stuff of legends. The misunderstanding engineered by Summer Phillips was one of many reasons that Maggie felt nothing but the purest strain of loathing for the woman.

But Maggie refused to let Summer and her shenanigans taint this second chance that she and Sam had. They had spent more than twenty years apart, and while Maggie would never ever regret her marriage to Charlie Gerber and the birth of her daughter, Laura, she couldn't help but wonder what would have happened to her and Sam if they hadn't broken up all those years ago.

Then again, she had to acknowledge that if her seventeen-year-old self had been truly sure of Sam, she never would have fallen for Summer's stunt. So maybe she and Sam were just destined to meet when they were older and wiser. She certainly hoped that was the cosmic plan, at any rate.

"What are you thinking about?" he asked.

"The past," she said.

Sam gave her a rueful glance. "And here I thought you might be pondering the meaning of all those one-word notes and roses you've been receiving."

"The ones you deny you've been sending?" Maggie asked. She dipped a bit of her corn bread into the sauce-slathered pork and popped it into her mouth.

"I refuse to say anything on the grounds I might incriminate myself," he said. As if to emphasize his point, he tucked into his meal with gusto.

"So, you have no idea what 'Maggie, will you please be my . . .' might end with?"

"Is that what the notes say?" he asked. He raised his eyebrows. "Wow, that could be anything."

"Really?" Maggie asked. "Given that tomorrow is Valentine's Day, I sort of figured the answer was obvious."

Sam frowned. "Maybe it's going to spell out 'be my pal,' or 'be my cleaning woman,' or 'be my'—"

He didn't get to finish, as Maggie threw her napkin at him and nailed him right in the forehead.

He grinned as he tossed the napkin back to her. "I'm just saying there are a myriad of possibilities."

"Uh-huh," Maggie said.

"But now that you mention it, tomorrow *is* Valentine's Day, and since we are officially a couple, I'm thinking we should do it up big to make up for all of the ones we've missed."

His blue eyes were so earnest, Maggie felt her throat get tight. She and Sam had been at odds for such a long time, it completely charmed her to have him so invested in their new relationship.

"Well, I don't know," she teased. "I think I have to wait and see what my final note says. I mean, I wouldn't want to commit to something and then have to cancel because the single most romantic gesture of my life ends in the phrase 'cleaning woman.'"

"'Single most romantic gesture,' huh?" he asked. He looked pretty pleased with himself.

"Hmm, so far," Maggie said. "But I fear it might take a nasty turn on me."

Sam laughed and then nodded. "I can appreciate your concern. Now, I'm not saying I know anything about these notes, and I can't confirm or deny what the last one might say, but I'm pretty sure you can risk dinner with me."

In that moment, Maggie felt as if she would risk everything for Sam Collins. Her heart, her mind, her soul. The realization stunned her. She hadn't thought falling in love in her forties could surpass the crazy first love of her youth, but it had. Somehow, she had fallen even harder for the big lunk the second time around.

"That sounds really nice," she said, hoping her voice did not betray the crazy happy dance her heart was doing in her chest.

"Excellent," he said. He looked equal parts relieved and eager. "I'll pick you up at the shop at five?"

It meant closing a bit early, but Maggie didn't really anticipate a great rush in the shop on the biggest date night of the year.

"I'll be there," she said. "I promise."

Sam looked at her from beneath his lashes. She had a feeling she knew what he was thinking.

Twenty-four years ago, the night before he was to leave for college, she had stood him up. They were supposed to meet in their usual spot on the town green, but after she had been tricked into thinking he was shagging Summer on the side, well, she'd been absolutely devastated, and ditched him.

Sam had shown up at her house an hour later, looking for her. Maggie refused to come out of the house. She refused to talk to him on the phone. She sent back the letters he wrote to her from college. By Halloween, Sam had stopped trying to contact her.

She wondered if it had been as bad for him as it had been for her. And what made it even worse is that he'd had no idea about the nasty trick Summer had played. It had taken Sam returning to St. Stanley for her to finally find out the truth. Frustration at her own gullibility, anger at Summer for the stunt she pulled, and guilt for how badly she'd treated Sam swamped her.

"After you left for school, I cried for a week straight," she said.

Sam reached across the table and put his hand over hers. "I will deny it if you ever tell anyone, but there were tears on my side, too."

Maggie gave him a small smile. "I'm sorry. I should have talked to you and told you what happened. It is probably the only major regret I have in my life to date."

"It's all right," he said. "We were young and stupid. I should have insisted that you tell me what happened, but I was too proud."

"And I was too stubborn," Maggie said.

"Let's never make those mistakes again," Sam said. He lifted Maggie's hand to his lips as if to seal the pact.

"I promise," Maggie said. "And I will be waiting for you tomorrow no matter what."

Or so she thought.

Chapter 4

"I'm sorry. Why are you here again?" Maggie asked.

Blair Cassidy stood in the middle of Maggie's shop. It was mid-afternoon and there had been a lull in customers. Maggie figured it was because most people had a hot date to get ready for that night.

The Good Buy Girls had been in earlier to give Maggie a consult on the outfit she should wear tonight. After rejecting a pale blue ingenue sort of dress with a Peter Pan collar and a poofy skirt, and passing on a red velvet dress low in the front with a slit up to—well, it was very high—they had all agreed that black and slinky was the way to go.

The dress in question was hanging in the storeroom waiting for her to put it on before Sam arrived. It was a curve-hugger with a flirty skirt and, paired with some gravity-defying heels, Maggie was pretty sure Sam would approve.

"I'm just checking out your selection of furniture," Blair said. She ran her hand over the back of the velvet love seat, which Maggie had picked up at a garage sale from the Fitzpatricks, who had sold off everything in order to move to their retirement home on the Carolina shore.

It was a vintage piece, and she knew that even Blair Cassidy could appreciate the carved wooden frame and delicate shape. She could tell Blair could find no fault with it, because she said nothing, as opposed to insulting her.

"Is there anything in particular you're looking for?" Maggie asked. She really wasn't interested, but she was attempting to be polite. It was a strain, but she was sure she would earn good karma points if she could just remain pleasant.

"Well, Summer doesn't carry furniture," Blair said. "Her interest is more in *high end* fashion, but I have this friend who is looking to consign some vintage fifties kitchen items."

Maggie decided to ignore the jab that her fashion sense was less than Summer's when, the last time she checked, Summer seemed to acquire her clothing from Playboy Bunny castoffs. Still, fifties kitchenware would be fabulous to display in the shop.

"What kind of items?" Maggie asked. She tried to make her tone one of bored semi-interest. She failed. The sane part of her brain was demanding to know why was she talking to this woman who she knew very well didn't like her and had designs on her man for her own daughter. Maggie tuned out the voice of reason as Blair listed the items.

"Franciscan Starburst, a complete set," Blair said. "A dining set of four aqua chairs and a matching Formica table, in mint condition; a vintage copper canister set; you know, stuff like that."

Maggie had to check her chin for drool. She simply loved fifties-style everything. She supposed it was reflected in her shop by the amount of items she carried that definitely bespoke the postwar heyday of the twentieth century.

"When would they need someone to consign the items for them?" Maggie asked. Again, she was striving to sound mildly interested. She could tell by the evil sparkle in Blair's eyes that she failed.

"Oh, right away," Blair said. "They're hoping to move as soon as possible."

"Who is it? Maybe I know them," Maggie said. "I have lived in St. Stanley all my life. There really isn't anyone I don't know at least in passing."

"No, you don't know them," Blair said. "They're not . . . Well, quite frankly, they're not your kind. They are in a different social circle than you."

"Meaning?" Maggie asked. She could feel her temper flare at the implied insult.

"They're just not very outgoing," Blair said. "That's all. They're introverts and don't go out much. Why? Whatever did you think I meant?"

She turned away from Maggie and studied herself in a nearby mirror. She smoothed her eyebrows with her index finger. Although gravity had started to show along her jawline, Blair still looked amazing for a woman who was several years into her AARP membership.

Maggie stared at her. Why was Blair really here? She had to be working an angle. There was no way that she cared about Maggie or Maggie's store, and she certainly would not feel obligated to help Maggie in any way.

"My friends are desperate. I told them I might know of someone who would be willing to take their things for them," Blair said. She said it as if it pained her to be sharing this information with Maggie.

Maggie crossed her arms over her chest. She wasn't sure what Blair was playing at, but she definitely didn't trust her.

"If you're thinking of me and my shop, I'd have to see the items before I could say whether I could carry them or not," Maggie said. She fully expected Blair to be pulling a scam by unloading her friends' junk on her.

"Of course," Blair said. "Since my friends are in a hurry, we could go now and you could see the items."

Maggie glanced around the shop. There was no one here, but she didn't like to close up on the off chance that a customer came by and thought she was flighty and unreliable.

Then again, vintage fifties stuff was hot, and it could be a huge score.

Blair was checking her phone. "Yes, my friend texts she'll only be available for the next hour."

Maggie sighed. She was very unhappy about this. The

thought of being stuck in a car with Blair was almost a deal breaker, but she had a couple of hours until her date and she really wasn't in a position to pass up something that had the potential to be a big seller. She could just picture the window display she could create with the items.

"All right," she said. "Wait here . . . please."

Maggie went into the small office that was at the back of the shop, adjacent to her storeroom. She grabbed her purse from her desk drawer and took her coat off of the coatrack. She found Blair looking at the display case where she kept vintage jewelry.

"See anything you like?" Maggie asked.

Blair looked at her in alarm, as if she were horrified that Maggie might think she was interested. It was true that most of Maggie's pieces were of the old-lady costume variety, but that did not mean they were of little value.

Maggie was always careful to look for signs of quality in costume jewelry, such as pronged settings, substantial weight, smooth plating and sparkling stones. Certain manufacturers were an instant buy as well. She always scooped up pieces by Eisenberg or Schiaparelli. In fact, she had recently sold a Schiaparelli brooch for two hundred dollars.

Blair wrinkled her nose at the case and Maggie figured she was allergic to anything that was not platinum and loaded with diamonds. Whatever.

"I'll drive," Maggie said. She wasn't sure why she was so insistent, but if she did score some things for the shop, she'd need her station wagon to haul them. Also, being in the driver's seat would make her feel as if she had control of the situation.

Blair nodded and walked out of the shop. Maggie turned the CLOSED sign on the door and locked it behind her. As she led the way to her car, she couldn't help feeling as if she was making a very bad mistake.

"Which way do I go?" Maggie asked.

Blair pulled her coat closely around her as if trying to shield herself from being contaminated by anything in Maggie's car. Maggie blew out a breath and waited for Blair to buckle herself in. Yes, there were some papers on the floor, and a few candy wrappers, as well as a couple of empty soda cans. Maggie had meant to pick these things up, but she'd forgotten.

"You want to go left on Main Street and all the way through town until you get to Route Twenty," Blair said.

"They live way out on Route Twenty?"

"Thereabouts," Blair said.

Maggie frowned. She had the feeling that Blair wasn't telling her something. She didn't know what, and she didn't have a good feeling about it.

The sky was gray and overcast. There was a definite chill in the air, so she cranked up the heater in her car. The center of town was quiet—again, because most people had something better to do tonight and weren't being dragged out into the cold just for a bargain.

She thought about her dress hanging in the storeroom and sighed. She considered her date with Sam, and she wondered if she was doing the right thing.

"If I remember right, my friend has quite a collection

of Art Deco cut glassware from the nineteen twenties," Blair said. "That might be popular in your quaint little shop."

Art Deco glassware? Fine, she would go. How could she not? She would check it out. If it was junk, she would make her excuses and leave. She had to assume that Blair was doing this because it suited her to help her friends, and she probably wanted Maggie to focus on furniture and home goods in her shop so Summer could have more of the local clothing market. Fine. Whatever.

"Does Summer know you're helping me?" Maggie asked.

"Oh, yes," Blair said. "She was quite enthusiastic about it."

Maggie gave her a sidelong look. They were leaving the center of town and were just a few miles from Route Twenty.

An alarm bell was going off in her head.

"Enthusiastic?" she asked. There was no way Summer would be happy for her unless it involved something painful for Maggie.

"Oh, yes," Blair said. "How did she put it? That's right, She said, 'I really hope Maggie drowns under all of that lame stuff.'"

"Well, that sounds like the Summer I know and love," Maggie said.

"Doesn't it though?" Blair asked. She sounded proud. "Her shop is really splendid. Have you been in to see it?"

"No," Maggie said.

"Really?" Blair asked. "Aren't you even curious?"

"No."

"Well, I suppose it is best to live in ignorance when you're not quite on the same level as someone else. That way your tender feelings won't get hurt."

"What the heck is that supposed to mean?" Maggie asked.

"Oh, here's our street," Blair said as gestured out the window.

Maggie slowed down and cut the wheel. Still, she was going a bit too fast, and the car bounced into the turn. Blair steadied herself by reaching out and grabbing the dashboard and gave Maggie a chastising look.

"You really should drive more carefully," she said. "But, of course, with your fiery temperament . . ."

"My fiery temperament?" Maggie sputtered. She almost pulled over the car, but another car was behind her, pushing her along. "Your daughter is a mean, twisted psychopath, and you say that I have a fiery temperament?"

Blair just looked at her with one eyebrow raised in haughty disdain, as if Maggie were doing nothing but proving her point.

Maggie forced deep breaths in through her nose and out through her mouth as she tried to calm down. She was not going to bicker with Blair about her daughter. Of course Blair was on Summer's side. She was her mother, and judging by her string of ex-husbands and penchant for tight clothing, Summer was the acorn who had not rolled far from the oak.

"I'm sorry," Maggie said. "I guess we shouldn't be talking about Summer, since we have such differing opinions of her personality and such."

That was the closest thing to an olive branch Maggie could offer. Unfortunately, she should have suspected that Blair would do exactly what Summer would have done—smack Maggie upside the head with it.

"You're right," Blair said. "I know it must be very hard for you to know that Sam has pined for Summer all these years and that you're just a sad substitute, but honestly, don't you think it's time you cut him loose so he could have the woman he truly belongs with?"

"What?" Maggie turned and stared at Blair hard before turning back to the road. "Are you kidding me?"

They were cruising along a sparsely populated stretch of road. The trees arched over them, their bare limbs reminding Maggie of skeletons reaching up from the grave as if trying to catch her and drag her down. She could have told them not to bother, since she seemed to have a specter of death sitting beside her.

Blair gave her a sympathetic shake of the head. "I know it's hard, but you need to accept the inevitable. You've already had your family. It's time you let Sam have his with a woman who hasn't already been there and done that."

Maggie blew out a breath, trying to contain her temper.

"Sam is not now nor was he ever in love with Summer. I'm sorry. I don't mean to be blunt, but honestly, both you and Summer need to stop chasing him. He's just not interested and, as for him wanting a family, well, that's just . . ." Maggie's voice trailed off as she lost her words. She really didn't know what to say about that.

Blair turned halfway in her seat and gave Maggie a

look that was full of pity. "Really? He's not? Then why is his squad car parked next to Summer's in front of that—oh dear, is that a motel?"

Maggie turned her head to look. Yes, that was Sam's car, and she recognized Summer's beside it. Instinct took over, and before she could think it through, she turned the wheel into the parking lot and stomped on the brakes, stopping her car right before it smashed into Sam's.

Chapter 5

"What have you done?" Maggie asked Blair. She was livid. "If you harmed one hair on that man's head, I will kick your butt!"

With that she slammed out of her car and stormed toward the open door of motel room number seven.

"Sam?" she cried. "Are you all right? They didn't knock you out or drug you, did they?"

She barged into the room with Blair right behind her, yelling, "You can't stop true love, Maggie! Sam has made his choice, and it's best for everyone involved if you just accept it."

Maggie stumbled to a halt just past the threshold. The sight that greeted her made her eyes bug in shock and horror. Unfortunately, Blair slammed into her back, projecting her into the room.

"Whoa!" Maggie said, and quickly averted her gaze, holding up her hand to block the view.

"What is *this*?" Blair screeched.

Maggie glanced through her fingers to see Blair standing with her hands on her hips, facing the bed, looking ready to do battle.

"Wild guess here, but it looks to be Tyler Fawkes in bed with your daughter, ma'am," Sam said from behind the hat he was using to shield his view. His eyes met Maggie's, and he grinned. "What? Did you think they kidnapped me?"

"It crossed my mind," she said. She moved to stand beside him and went up on tiptoe to kiss his cheek. "I'm glad you're okay. I really was not up to snatching the hair off Summer's head for harming my man."

" 'Your man,' huh?" Sam asked. "I do like that."

"Summer Phillips, you get out of that bed right now!" Blair demanded.

"Hey, now, if you all could just give us a minute?" Tyler spoke up, but Blair turned on him.

"Do not speak," she demanded.

"But—" he protested.

"No!" Blair roared. She reached over and yanked Summer out of the bed. Maggie was relieved to see that Summer was dressed, sort of, in a slinky slip type of thing.

"You had one thing to do," Blair was yelling at Summer now. "One thing, and you screwed it up. This is why you are such a loser. How hard is it to seduce one man?

You got the legs, the boobs—clearly it's the brains you're lacking."

"I tried, but—" Summer began to protest.

The cold air from outside was billowing into the room, and Summer shivered. Blair was pacing, looking like she wasn't sure who she wanted to paddle more—Summer or Tyler or both. When Summer's teeth began to chatter, Tyler rose up out of the bed—he was still in his undershorts, thank heavens—and wrapped a blanket around Summer's shoulders.

Tyler was a big man in both height and girth. He was also pretty hairy, with a full beard and a pelt of chest hair that looked like something only found in the zoo next to a sign that said DO NOT FEED THE BEARS. Despite his forbidding appearance, when he looked down at Summer it was with a tenderness that bespoke more than lust; it was a look of genuine caring and concern.

Maggie realized that Tyler was in love with Summer. The poor guy. Falling for a woman who, as far as Maggie could tell, was incapable of human emotions—that was some serious bad luck.

"It's not Summer's fault," Tyler said. "I saw her driving out here and I followed her, well, because I've missed her and I wanted to talk to her. I wanted to see if maybe we could get back together."

"I'm sure you wanted to *talk*," Blair spat. Then she turned on Summer. "What's the matter with you? Are you stupid or slow or both? Why would you go for him?" She waved a dismissive hand at Tyler. "When you're supposed to be seducing *that* man!"

She pointed at Sam, who looked immediately alarmed.

"Say what?" he asked. "I came here because someone called in a disturbance, and then I found you two, which explained all the noise."

His face flushed a faint shade of pink, and since Sam never blushed, Maggie could only imagine what he had walked in on. Oh, dear!

"Piecing it all together," Maggie said to Sam, "I'd say, Summer was supposed to seduce you while Blair conned me into supposedly coming out here to look at some items for my shop; we were supposed to walk in on you two; I would be suitably devastated; and we'd break up, thus paving the way for you and Summer to be together forever."

Sam's eyebrows shot up to his hairline. Maggie looked at Blair.

"How am I doing so far?"

"I will not dignify that ridiculous story with an answer," she said.

"Probably, that's just as well," Sam said with a glower. "Or I'd have to cite you for making a false report. Didn't we already do this song and dance once? Did you really think we'd fall for it again?"

"Since it worked so well the first time, I'm sure they were counting on it," Maggie said.

"Hey, now, hold up," Tyler sputtered as he tried to yank on his pants. "What are they talking about, Summer? Is this true?"

"No, sugar, it's all just a horrible misunderstanding," Summer said. She was looking at Tyler with pleading eyes, but it didn't work.

"I can't believe you'd do that to them or to us," he said. He frowned at her. "You were really going to bust them up by seducing him? That's just cold and mean."

"No, Tyler, wait. I can explain," Summer pleaded. She put her hand on his arm to stop him from leaving.

He shook her off, looking hurt and disappointed. "I'm sorry, darling, but you're not the girl I thought you were."

With that, Tyler grabbed his shirt and jacket and stormed out of the room.

Maggie would have thought he'd slam the door in a temper, but Tyler shut it quietly behind him, making his departure seem all the more serious and condemning.

Summer had been Maggie's nemesis since childhood. Maggie thought she'd enjoy seeing Summer put in her place, but Summer was the picture of misery, and Maggie was stunned to find she actually felt sorry for her.

"If you care about him, go after him," Maggie said. "Trust me on this."

"You stay out of it!" Blair snapped. She turned to Summer and said, "Don't even think about following that man. You put one toe outside this room and I will disown you."

"But I lo—" Summer began to protest, but her mother cut her off.

"No, you don't," Blair said. "You can do so much better than that no-account trailer trash."

"Tyler's not—" Maggie protested, but Blair cut her off, too.

"And *you* can bet I won't be taking you to see my friend's collectibles either," Blair said.

"See?" Maggie asked. "Now that's where I should have caught on. A viper like you doesn't have any friends!"

"How dare you?" Blair sucked in a breath, but Maggie didn't care.

"Oh, I dare. You might want to be nicer to Tyler," she said. "As far as I can tell, he's your only ride home."

With that, Maggie spun on her heel and stormed out the door. She could hear Sam trying to choke back a laugh as he followed her.

Once they were in the parking lot, the chilly February wind did wonders to cool Maggie's ire. She pulled her coat more tightly about herself as she stomped to her car.

"I can't believe I fell for it," she muttered.

Sam jogged to catch up to her and caught her hand in his. "Hey, Maggie, hold up."

"Sorry," she said. She slowed her pace to match his. "I am just so angry. I can't believe I fell for Blair's line about having friends with old fifties kitchen memorabilia. I am such an idiot."

"No, you're not," he said. They stopped beside her car and he tugged her into his arms. "You're a savvy small business owner who thought she was onto a score."

"But what if Tyler hadn't followed Summer out here?" Maggie asked. "What if I had walked into their trap?"

Sam leaned back to study her face. "What if you had walked in on Summer and me alone? What do you think you would have found?"

An image of Summer from their high school days

having a jolly good time with a guy wearing Sam's football jersey flashed through her mind. *Gross!*

At her silence, Sam continued, "I can tell you what you would have found—me hiding in the bathroom."

Maggie burst out laughing. The idea that Sam would hide from Summer on the make was ludicrous and lovely.

"Thank you. I thought you might be hiding under the bed, but the bathroom makes more sense," she said. She glanced at the closed motel room door. "I have to be honest. For the first time ever, I actually felt sorry for Summer. Her mother was so cruel to her."

"Me, too," Sam said. "Her mother is a horror. I really thought Blair was an over-involved helicopter mother, but clearly she has her own agenda, and Summer's happiness is not on it."

"This whole episode explains a lot," Maggie said. "About why Summer is the way she is. I always wondered what made her so mean and now I know it's in her DNA. She is either genetically predisposed for cruelty or she just doesn't know any better."

"And that is another thing I love about you, Maggie Gerber," he said. "You have a big heart."

Sam leaned forward and kissed her, and Maggie felt as if all was right with her world again.

"Oh, hey," Sam said as he stepped back. "Don't you have a date tonight?"

"I do," Maggie said. "At five."

She glanced at her watch. It was a quarter to four. She'd never make it back in time to dress and change. Oh, no!

Sam smiled at her. "It's okay. I think your date is running behind as well. Want to roll it back to five thirty?"

"Ish," Maggie amended. "Five thirty-ish. That's a fifteen-minute buffer, for the uninitiated."

"Five thirty-ish it is," he said. "See you at the shop."

Maggie gave him a quick kiss and climbed into her car. She saw Sam wander over to the far side of the lot, where Tyler was sitting in his truck. She wondered what sort of pep talk Sam would give to Tyler. He'd certainly suffered a humiliating blow at the hands of Blair Cassidy.

This all could have gone so horribly awry. She couldn't help but be grateful that Summer and her mother's scheme hadn't worked this time.

Chapter 6

Sam arrived at the shop at five thirty on the dot. Maggie was relieved that she hadn't needed the ish factor after all. When she opened the door to let him in, he looked suitably awestruck by her slinky black dress and high heels.

"Wow," he said. "You are gorgeous."

Maggie felt her face get hot as she took in his charcoal gray suit, light blue dress shirt and burgundy necktie.

"You clean up pretty well yourself," she said.

He grinned at her. "Deputy Wilson threatened to tase me if I wore my uniform."

Maggie laughed. She could see Dot doing that. Sam lifted her coat off the back of a chair and held it open for her. Maggie slipped it on and felt his hands rest on her shoulders with the familiarity of someone who was becoming intimately acquainted with her person.

Was this really them? She caught sight of their reflection in the window glass and her breath caught. They were a couple; a couple that was dating, going out to dinner and, dare she think it, falling in love again. She wondered what her brokenhearted seventeen-year-old self would have thought if she had known the future held this moment in store.

"What are you thinking?" he asked.

Maggie felt her face grow warm. Did she have the nerve to tell him? Yes, she did.

"Just that I wish I'd known when I was seventeen that I'd have the opportunity to fall in love with you again," she said.

Sam's blue eyes met hers in a look that was more than the scorching heat of chemistry, although there was plenty of that. It was a tangible connection of the soul-deep kind, the twined vines of friendship, love and passion. Wow.

"I wish I'd known, too," he said. "Realizing I'd get to call you my girl again would have helped me get through some very dark days."

He kissed her, and to Maggie it felt as if there was a promise tucked in it.

"Ready to go?" he asked when he stepped back.

"Yes, definitely," she said.

Sam led the way out the door, waiting while Maggie locked up. He was driving his personal vehicle tonight and not a squad car. Maggie hoped that this meant they could have a crime-free evening.

"Who's on patrol tonight?" she asked as he settled her into his SUV.

"The rookies," he said. "Deputy Wilson threatened to tase them, too, if they called me before they called her."

"She is determined that you have a night off," Maggie said.

"So it would seem," Sam said. "I have to admit, it will be nice to eat in a restaurant and not be worried that I'm going to have to run out halfway through the meal."

"So, we're going to a restaurant?" Maggie asked.

"Voltaire's, if that's okay?" Sam asked.

"Okay?" Maggie asked. "It's the finest French restaurant in the county. I've always wanted to eat there."

"I'd heard something like that," Sam said.

"Talked to Ginger, did you?"

"Well, I wasn't a crackerjack detective on the Richmond force for nothing," he said. "I do need to make one stop first."

Maggie nodded. That was fine. Everything was fine. She'd be just as happy to eat at a highway truck stop, so long as she was with Sam.

They hadn't driven far when Sam pulled over to the curb on the town green. He turned in his seat and said, "Come on, I want to show you something."

He got out of the car and hurried around to open the door for Maggie. She noticed the center of town was quiet as she slipped out of the car and into the cold night air.

Sam took her hand and walked her down the path that led through the barren green. The gazebo where the local geriatric jazz band put on weekly summer concerts was lit up with strings of white and red lights.

"Look at that," Maggie said. "Someone decorated the gazebo."

She glanced at Sam, and even in the dim light of the night she could see his face flush with embarrassment.

"You?" she asked.

He gave a self-conscious chuckle and put his free hand on the back of his neck. "Yeah."

"Oh, Sam," Maggie said. "It's beautiful."

Together they climbed the steps. The red and white lights cast a pretty glow all around the wooden structure. The gazebo was legendary in St. Stanley as the place where all the couples came to pledge their love. It had been built over a hundred years ago. Maggie figured there probably wasn't an original board left in the place, but the town had faithfully, some might say scrupulously, maintained its original look, because it was the heart of St. Stanley.

The story went that Stewart Devon, a wandering carpenter, blew into St. Stanley and was hired to build the gazebo. While he worked, he fell in love with the mayor's daughter. Of course, the mayor forbade his daughter, Anastasia, to have anything to do with the lowly carpenter. So Stewart built the gazebo as slowly as he could until the mayor threatened to throw him in jail if he didn't finish.

Reluctantly, Stewart finished the gazebo. The town held a party to celebrate its completion, and Stewart prepared to leave St. Stanley. Mysteriously, the gazebo burnt down that night. A witness claimed that Anastasia was the one to burn it down.

The mayor didn't want his daughter arrested for arson and so asked Stewart to take her away with him. Stewart said no. He knew that Anastasia loved St. Stanley and didn't want to leave and so he made a pact with the town that if he rebuilt the gazebo they would not arrest Anastasia for arson. The town agreed and the couple was the first to be married in the gazebo. Mr. and Mrs. Stewart Devon lived out their days in St. Stanley, having three children and seven grandchildren, and the gazebo became a sacred spot to all St. Stanley couples.

Doc Franklin had gotten down on one knee and proposed to his wife Alice here. During a summer concert, Roger Lancaster had first asked Ginger out on the steps. And Sam Collins, well, when he was eight years old, he'd been on the receiving end of a bloody nose from seven-year-old Maggie O'Brien, years before she became Maggie Gerber, for teasing her about her favorite sparkly pink shoes.

Sam turned Maggie to face him, holding her hands in his.

"The night before I left for college, I had it all planned out. I wanted to bring you right here, with flowers and music, and tell you that I loved you and ask you to wait for me."

"Oh, Sam," Maggie felt her heart squeeze tight. "I'm so—"

"No, don't be," Sam said. "I didn't know it then, but it

played out the way it was supposed to. You were destined to marry Charlie and have Laura and become the amazing woman that you are. And I was supposed to go to Richmond and become a detective. I loved my career, and I wouldn't be the man that I am if I hadn't chosen that path."

"But this is so wonderful," Maggie said. "And it hurts me to know that you did this for me back then, and I shut the door in your face. Gah, I'm a horrible person."

Sam lifted her chin, forcing her gaze to meet his. "No, you're not. Honestly, Maggie, I don't think we were supposed to be together until now. We were both pretty hotheaded and stubborn. Well, more you than me," he teased. Maggie didn't argue because it was true. "I think we both needed to live a little and grow up a lot so we could truly appreciate what we have between us."

"Thank you," Maggie said. Her voice was rough, as she had to force her words past the lump in her throat. "For all of this, and for letting us have a do-over."

Sam let go of her hands and crossed the gazebo to take a single red rose out of a box with a note.

Maggie smiled when she took the flower and the note from him. She opened the card but the note was blank. She flipped it over and then glanced at Sam in question. He smiled and then held up one hand. From it dangled a diamond-encrusted heart on a golden chain.

"Valentine," he said. "Maggie, will you be my valentine?"

Maggie swallowed the lump in her throat, which naturally made a tear slip out of the corner of her eye. Sam wiped it away with the gentlest touch. Then she grinned and nodded.

"Yes, most definitely," she said. "I'll be your valentine so long as you promise to be mine."

"Always," Sam said.

He moved to stand behind her and fastened the necklace around her throat. Maggie fingered the heart and watched it sparkle in the light. It was perfect.

"There is just one thing you need to know," she said. "If things had gone differently that night, I would have told you I loved you, too, and I would have waited. In fact, I feel as if I've been waiting for you for a very long time. I love you, Sam Collins."

The smile Sam gave her was one she would carry with her always. It was him at his most boyish, just like when they were teens. She treasured that look. When he kissed her, she knew they had finally done it. They had healed the old hurts and laid to rest the ghosts of their past.

Dinner was perfect. The food. The wine. The company. Maggie couldn't remember when she'd had such a magical evening. She gave Sam his gift after dinner. She had used her connections in the resale world and gotten him a signed jersey for his beloved Ravens. Sam was thrilled. He was also a good storyteller, talking about his life in Richmond, but he was also a wonderful listener, asking her questions about her life in St. Stanley and marveling at how she'd managed on her own after Charlie had died.

Over the past few months, they had each shared snippets of their lives apart, but somehow, after their time in the gazebo, it was as if a final barrier had been removed. The stories they shared now were more personal and more honest. Maggie felt as if they knew it was okay. There was nothing, no secret they couldn't share, that would drive the other away. It was a remarkable place to be in after all these years.

Maggie felt like she could sit in the glow of the candlelight, drinking in the sight of Sam sitting across from her, for hours, days, quite possibly weeks, and never get tired of him, of them. Yes, they both had the crinkly lines of age at the corners of their eyes, and gray hair was just beginning to sprout, but she couldn't help but feel they had their whole lives ahead of them.

They were just leaving the restaurant when Maggie's phone chimed. She wondered if it was Laura calling from college to ask about her date. She surreptitiously pulled her phone out of her purse and checked the display as they walked to the door.

The number was Ginger's. Now, she knew her BFF was curious about her date, but she didn't think she'd be calling and interrupting unless something had happened.

"It's Ginger," she said.

"You take it," Sam said. "I'll get our coats."

He made his way to the coat check and Maggie answered the phone.

"Hello," Maggie said.

"You're not naked, are you?" Ginger asked.

"What? No!" Maggie said. "We're just leaving Voltaire's."

"Oh, good, Roger said not to call because I might be

interrupting . . . *you know*," Ginger said. Then she giggled.

Maggie rolled her eyes. She felt as if they were still in high school. "Clearly, you're not interrupting *you know*, so what's happening?"

"Michael just called," Ginger said. Now her voice was straight-up serious. "Joanne is in labor. They are on their way to the hospital right now."

"Get out!" Maggie said. "But this is early, isn't it?"

"Yes," Ginger said.

Maggie could hear the concern in her friend's voice.

"Claire and Pete have already left for the hospital, and Roger and I are on our way now," Ginger said. "I can keep you posted with texts if you want."

Sam returned with their coats over his arm.

"Oh, no," Maggie said. "Good Buy Girls stick together through it all, especially birth. I'll meet you at the hospital."

Sam raised his eyebrows and mouthed, *Joanne?* Maggie nodded at him and he blew out a breath as if he were nervous, too.

"But it's your first Valentine's Day with Sam," Ginger protested. "You should spend it alone together."

"There'll be more Valentine's Days for us," Maggie said.

Sam smiled at her as if he liked the sound of that, and Maggie almost forgot who she was talking to and why.

Sam took the phone from her hand. "We'll see you at the hospital, Ginger," he said.

Whatever she answered made him chuckle as he hung

up. Sam held open her coat and Maggie shrugged it on. He then handed her phone back, and Maggie tucked it into her purse.

As he walked her out to the car, Maggie noticed that he had a faraway look in his eyes. She suddenly felt very guilty for ending their date at the hospital.

"I'm really sorry about this," she said. "But Joanne and Michael have been trying for so long. I just feel like she needs all the support she can get, especially with the baby coming this early."

Sam put an arm around her shoulders and pulled her close.

"Don't apologize," he said. "Of course you need to be with Joanne. Besides, it's a baby. How cool is that?"

Maggie looked at him and saw the happy light in his eyes. Oh no, he liked babies! Panic started to thump through her. Maybe he wanted some of his own. Maybe he wanted them with her!

Chapter 7

"Come on," he said. "I have my siren in the car. I can get us there in no time."

Sure enough, he slapped a siren on the roof and punched the gas. They were pulling into the hospital lot before Maggie had processed all that was going through her head.

He parked in the visitor's section and they hurried across the lot to the main entrance. A lovely older woman was working the information desk, and she smiled at them.

"Visiting hours are about to end," she said.

"We're looking for the maternity ward," Maggie said.

"Right down the hall," the lady said. "Follow the yellow line and it will take you to the elevators. You want to get off on the third floor and go to your right."

"Thank you," Maggie said.

Sam had already grabbed her hand and they were jogging for the elevators. When they got off on the third floor and turned right, they passed a large waiting room. Ginger and Roger and Pete and Claire were all sitting there. Maggie could tell by everyone's dressed-up duds that they'd all been enjoying lovely Valentine's Days of their own.

"Maggie!" Ginger and Claire both hurried toward her.

"Is there any word?" Maggie asked. "Is Joanne okay?"

"She and Michael have been back there for a while," Claire said. "No word as yet."

"Look at me," Ginger said. She held out her hands to show they were shaking. "I am a nervous wreck."

"There's no need," Maggie said. "Joanne is one tough cookie, she's from New York, she'll be fine."

And she hoped by declaring it emphatically she could make it so.

"You're right," Claire said. "She's going to be just fine."

The three of them were silent for a moment. Maggie noticed that Sam had sat right down with Roger and Pete where they were watching a basketball game on the flat-screen television bolted to the wall.

Men! Didn't they know they were in a high alert sort of situation?

She glanced back at her friends and noticed Ginger's gaze on the sparkly heart around Maggie's neck.

"So, what was the final word of the week?" Ginger asked.

Maggie smiled. "Valentine. He asked me to be his valentine."

Claire sighed. "It sounds like it was very romantic."

"It was," Maggie said. "Sort of made up for all the ones we've missed over the years. How about you? Did you have a nice date with Pete?"

"Oh, we haven't even started yet," she said. "I had to close the library. He had just picked me up when we got the call."

"What about you and Roger?" Maggie asked.

Ginger smiled. "We finished our dinner date and were headed home to make certain none of the boys got up to mischief while we were gone."

"Your boys are wonderful. They would never—" Claire began, but Ginger cut her off.

"Oh no, teenage boys and their hormones must never be trusted. I swear their brains short out and they are incapable of overriding their impulses. Roger and I maintain a state of constant vigilance," she said.

"It's true," Maggie said. "The decision-making skills are just not there yet. I was the same way with Laura."

"This is one more reason why I don't have the stamina to have a child," Claire said. "It must be exhausting."

Maggie frowned. Yes, it was, and it was definitely not for the faint of heart.

"Hey, you okay?" Ginger jostled her arm.

"Me?" Maggie asked. "Yeah, I'm just . . . uh . . . thinking about all that Joanne and Michael have ahead of them. You know, midnight feedings, potty training, the first time the baby gets sick, teaching them to read and ride a bike, getting into a good college . . . Good grief, it never ends."

"Bless their hearts," Ginger said.

"Indeed," Maggie said.

Her gaze strayed back over to Sam. He was half reclined in his seat, laughing at some joke Pete had made. She could just see a sleeping baby sacked out on his chest. The thought warmed and chilled her at the same time.

As if he sensed her stare, he glanced over at her, and his smile was accompanied by a mischievous wink. Maggie smiled back, but it felt forced. She turned to her friends.

"Does anyone know what Joanne was craving for the past few weeks?" Claire asked. "I read that depending upon what a woman craves, you can sometimes determine the sex of the baby."

"Oh, but no," Ginger said. "Honey, you are just going to have to wait like the rest of us. Besides, Joanne has craved everything from coconut and caramel to root beer and raspberries."

"Raspberries, huh," Claire said. "I'll have to look that one up."

Clearly, she was not willing to give up her quest for the answer to Baby Claramotta's gender.

Abruptly, the door to the waiting room swung open and Michael and Joanne strode into the room. They were both upright and walking, with no bundle of joy in their arms.

"You're still pregnant!" Claire squawked. "Shouldn't you be lying down with your feet in stirrups by now?"

Joanne gave her a wan smile. "Sorry. It was a false alarm."

"Well, false labor at any rate," Michael said. He shouldered her hospital bag while keeping his other arm wrapped protectively about Joanne.

"I think the baby just wants to make sure we know what we're doing," Joanne said.

Sam, Roger and Pete joined the group.

"Darn, and I was really hoping you'd name the baby Valentine, too," Pete said.

Claire laughed while the others cringed.

"What? It could be worse," he said. "How about Cupid?"

They all began to walk out of the hospital together. Maggie could hear Pete offering up more names behind her.

"Arrow? Eros?"

She caught up to Joanne and asked, "Are you okay?"

"Yeah, just tired and a little disappointed," Joanne said. "I mean I know it would have been early and it's better that the baby has a few more weeks to build up its immunity and all, but . . ."

"You want to meet him or her?" Maggie asked.

"Yes," Joanne said. Her eyes were shining. "I really, really do."

"It'll happen before you know it," Ginger said as she muscled her way between Michael and Joanne.

"Promise?" Claire asked from Maggie's other side. "Because I don't know about you, but it is driving me plumb crazy not knowing what we're having."

"*We're* having?" Joanne repeated. Then she laughed. "I like that. Thank you all for being here. It means a lot."

"Where else would we be?" Ginger asked.

"Seriously, I haven't been stockpiling cloth diapers for months for nothing," Claire said.

"Go home and rest," Maggie said. "Because after the baby comes, you won't have another chance for a very long time."

Joanne hugged each of them when they stopped by her car.

Michael opened the back door and tossed the hospital bag in, then he opened the passenger door for Joanne.

Once she climbed in, he closed the door behind her.

He shook hands with the men and hugged the women. "Thanks, all. We'll keep you posted."

"Please do," Sam said. "And if you need a police escort at crunch time, just let me know. I've got connections."

They banged knuckles and Michael got into his car. They stood in a group, waving, as Michael and Joanne headed home.

"Well, I don't know about the rest of you, but my nerves are shot," Pete said. "There's a band playing at the Daily Grind, and I hear that place has some of the best java and chai tea in town. Who's in?"

Ginger looked at Roger. "Do you suppose we can trust the boys?"

"I will call and threaten them in my big daddy voice," he said. "Then I'll double down with a guilt bomb about how I never get to take their mama out and I'm taking her tonight and expect no shenanigans."

"I like it," Ginger said. "We're in."

Sam pulled Maggie close and wiggled his eyebrows. "How about it? I bet we could slow dance."

Maggie grinned. "That is too good of an offer to refuse." She turned to the others. "We're in, too."

The band playing at the coffee shop was one that specialized in cover songs, and tonight they were pulling out all of the romantic stops.

Staff and customers alike greeted Pete like their favorite uncle, and Maggie was pleased to see that most of them acknowledged Claire as his significant other. A jovial extrovert who was always quick with a joke, Pete seemed to balance Claire's shy bookishness.

"They really are a perfect couple," Ginger said to Maggie as they took a table toward the back while Roger and Sam paused to chat with one of their poker buddies.

A waitress came by and Maggie was amazed to find that, just like Ginger ordering for Roger, she knew what to order for Sam as well.

"So, how are things going?" Ginger asked. "How was it with Sam? Did you have a nice dinner? What did you talk about? Any discussion about the future?"

"It was amazing," Maggie said.

"And?"

"There needs to be an and after 'amazing'?"

"Details, girlfriend. I want details," Ginger said.

"Why?" Maggie teased. "It sounds to me like you and Roger have enough going on that you wouldn't need to live vicariously through my dating life."

"There's always room for inspiration. But seriously, I just want to know that things are progressing in the proper fashion."

"They are," Maggie assured her. "Everything is just fine."

"But . . ." Ginger prodded.

"No buts," Maggie said.

"Oh, puhleeze," Ginger said. "If ever there was anyone in the history of the world who overthought things it is you, and I know you have started second-guessing your relationship with Sam. It's what you do."

"I do not," Maggie protested.

"Then what was that funny look I saw on your face when you were looking at Sam in the waiting room?" Ginger asked.

"You saw that?" Maggie asked.

"Uh-huh," Ginger said.

"Okay, fine," Maggie said. "It's not a big deal. It just occurred to me that perhaps Sam might want one."

"Want one what?" Ginger asked. "You're going to have to be more specific. It's Valentine's Day, and my mind is ripe with naughty ideas."

Maggie laughed. No wonder Ginger and Roger were still happily married after all these years. Ginger had a deliciously deviant side.

"Mind out of the gutter, please," Maggie said. She leaned forward and lowered her voice. "A baby. After our conversation in the shop the other day, it occurred to me that Sam might want a baby."

Ginger pursed her lips and her eyes went round. "Okay, I did not see that coming."

"Neither did I," Maggie said. "What do I do if he does? What if he wants the house, the wife, the two kids, and a minivan?"

"Minivans are highly underrated vehicles," Ginger said. "You really can't beat the practicality—"

Maggie gave her a dark look.

"Okay, then. Worry about it when he says he does," Ginger said. "First, you need to find out what his thoughts are on the subject. A conversation you probably should have had before you started playing with fire, if you know what I mean."

Maggie sighed. "We're in our forties. Honestly, I was so swept up in us, I didn't really think about it."

"Uh-oh, they're having a huddle," Roger said to Sam as they joined them.

Ginger and Maggie broke apart and flashed blinding grins at their men in an attempt to make it look like they hadn't been talking about one of them, which of course they had. "No, no huddle," Ginger said. Then she gave Roger a seductive smile that made him audibly gulp. "But if you were looking for a huddle, I'd be happy to give you one on the dance floor."

Roger held out his hand and helped Ginger to her feet. "Lead the way, pretty lady."

Sam took the seat that Ginger had vacated. He leaned in close and nuzzled Maggie's neck. "I like this."

"Like what?" she asked. Her voice was breathier than

she would have liked. How did he do that? Sam chuckled, and she knew he'd heard it.

"Being out, being a couple, with you," he said. "I feel like the luckiest guy in the world."

"Me, too," Maggie said. "Well, except for the guy part. I feel like the luckiest gal in the world."

She met his gaze and there was the same magic that had been between them from the time they were squabbling kids, hormonal teens, distant adults, and now as a couple. In fact, she was pretty sure the spark between them was hotter than ever.

"Pardon me. I hate to interrupt," a voice said. "But I think we need to have a talk."

Maggie glanced past Sam and saw Bruce Cassidy, Blair's husband and Summer's stepfather, standing by their table, and he did not look happy.

Chapter 8

"Mr. Cassidy," Maggie said. She glanced quickly at Sam, who rose to his feet.

"Call me Bruce," he said, and shook the hand that Sam extended.

"Sam. Sam Collins. And you've met Maggie," Sam said as he gestured for Bruce to take a seat.

"Briefly," Bruce said. He rubbed a hand over his eyes and Maggie noticed that he looked tired. He was clean-shaven, his gray hair was combed and his navy blue suit was impeccable, but his face had the drawn look of a man who had been in an argument and lost.

"It's good to see you again," he said.

"You, too," Maggie said. She glanced around the coffee shop. She didn't see either Blair or Summer. She couldn't believe they'd miss an opportunity to mess up her Valentine's Day; not willingly, at any rate.

"You're alone?" she asked.

"Yup," he said. His voice was a resigned drawl. "That's what happens when the womenfolk gang up on you. You spend the hearts and flowers day locked out of your house."

"Been there." Sam cringed and gave Maggie a sidelong glance she chose to ignore.

Bruce grunted. "I imagine you have. Of course, this is after I spent the better part of the evening listening to the events that occurred at a seedy motel on the outskirts of town."

Sam and Maggie exchanged a look. Maggie wanted to laugh but it seemed bad form in front of Bruce. She saw Sam's lips twitch, and she figured he was struggling as well.

"Sorry about that," Sam said. "It was an unfortunate incident."

"Tactful of you to put it like that," Bruce said. "The truth is Blair has gotten it into her very stubborn head that you should be dating her daughter, and I have to tell you, I'm afraid she'll stop at nothing to make it so."

"What are you saying?" Sam asked.

"Simply put, when Blair gets a bug up her bazoo, it is virtually impossible to distract the woman, even with something sparkly and shiny."

His obvious exasperation made Maggie smile. "Well, at least now I know where Summer gets it from."

Bruce frowned. "Yeah, poor kid. Her mother is pretty

hard on her. I think it comes out of Blair's own insecurities. Still, I can't imagine always having to be the best, the brightest, the most beautiful. That's a hell of thing to make a kid live up to."

Maggie nodded. She had a sudden urge to call her mother and thank her for just loving her for who she was even when she hadn't been very lovable, which during her teen years had been pretty often.

"Hopefully, after today, things will calm down," Sam said.

"We can always hope," Bruce said. He sounded doubtful though. "Listen, I don't want to hold up your romantic evening. I just wanted to make sure we were all on the same page. You two enjoy yourselves, and I'll see what I can do to find my wife a new and different hobby."

"We'd appreciate it," Sam said.

The two men shook hands and Bruce ambled out of the coffee shop and into the night. He had the hunched-over walk of a defeated man. But then he paused just outside the door, and Maggie watched as he turned up the collar of his coat against the nighttime chill. He stiffened his spine and tipped his chin up as if daring someone to try and sucker punch him. He strode down the sidewalk with a purposeful step before disappearing around the corner.

"What do you make of that?" Maggie asked Sam.

"The man has his hands full. I wish him all the luck in the world reining Blair in," Sam said.

The waitress stopped by the table with their drinks, and Sam pulled out his wallet to pay, but she waved him away.

"Mr. Cassidy already paid for it all," she said. "He said it was the least he could do."

"Oh, wasn't that nice?" Maggie asked.

"Poor guy probably spends his whole life paying people to forgive his wife's bad behavior," Sam said. Then he looked at Maggie and took her hand in his. "Have I told you lately how much I love you?"

"Yes," she said as she leaned forward and kissed him. "But you can say it as much as you want. I never get tired of hearing it. I love you, too."

"Oh, please, get a room," Roger said as he and Ginger joined them.

Sam leaned close to Maggie and whispered, "I like that idea."

Maggie felt a thrill course through her and smiled back at him. "Let's skip the slow dance. Your place or mine?"

"Marshall Dillon is waiting at my place," he said.

"Your place it is." Maggie loved that cat, and not just because he'd saved her life in the past, but because he was the world's greatest snuggler, second to Sam. She pushed their hot chocolates with extra whipped cream in front of Roger and Ginger. "A bonus round for you two."

They rose from their seats as one and Sam threw a hurried "Have a great night!" over his shoulder as he hauled Maggie out of the coffee shop.

"Fun night last night?" Ginger asked. She was standing in front of the long floor mirror by the dress section in Maggie's shop. She was holding up a lime green broomstick skirt with sparkly beads sewn on the hem and she turned this way and that so the beads could catch the light.

"Yep, how about you?" Maggie asked.

"When we got home, all four boys were accounted for and not a hoochie mama in sight," Ginger said. She sounded relieved, and Maggie laughed.

"I didn't think there were that many hoochie mamas in St. Stanley," she said.

"Oh, you would be surprised," Ginger said. "I'm all for women being liberated and getting equal pay for equal work, but I wouldn't want a boy calling or texting my daughter fifteen times a day, and I don't like girls who do that to my boys either."

"It's that fine line between crushing and stalking," Maggie agreed.

"Some girls need a little help with the definition and a quick instruction on healthy boundaries," Ginger said. She had fire in her eyes, and Maggie had the feeling the unfortunate parents of one young girl would be getting a call from Ginger in the near future.

"Has there been any word from Joanne?" Ginger asked as she hung the skirt back up and moved to join Maggie by the counter.

"Not that I've heard," she said. "False labor does seem cruel at this juncture, doesn't it?"

"It does," Ginger said. "I don't know who is more eager at this point, Joanne to finally hold her baby or Claire to know what sex the baby is."

"Between you and me," Maggie said, "what's your guess?"

"Boy," Ginger said. "I always pick boy because four out of four times, I was right."

"Good enough," Maggie said. "I haven't been able to get a feeling one way or the other, so I'm going for healthy."

The front door to the shop opened and three older ladies came in. Ginger glanced from them to Maggie and said, "Looks like you're needed. I'll catch you later."

Maggie waved as Ginger departed and then came around the counter to greet her customers.

"Good afternoon, ladies, can I help you find anything?"

"Hats, dear. Do you have any hats?" Mrs. Oliver asked.

Maggie knew her as a patient of Doc Franklin's from when she used to do his books.

"Are you looking for anything in particular, Mrs. Oliver?" Maggie asked.

"Well, something dressy," she said. "We've decided to take the shuttle bus over to Dumontville and have afternoon tea at the Anderson Hotel, and we want to do it right."

"Oh, that sounds lovely," Maggie said. "I have a few hats over here, left over from last spring's wedding season. Why don't you take a look?"

Maggie led Mrs. Oliver and her two companions over to a hat rack in the back of the shop. She had noticed more and more people had been coming in looking for hats. She wondered if their popularity was on the rise. She'd have to see what she could find on sale post–wedding season this year. A window display of spring hats could be fun and lucrative.

"Oh, look at that one," one of the ladies said to Mrs. Oliver. "That would match your Sunday suit perfectly."

Maggie left them to admire their reflections in the mirror. It really would be fabulous if hats made a comeback in the fashion world.

The door opened and Maggie glanced up with her "greet the customer" smile firmly in place.

"Good morning, how can I . . . Oh, it's you," she said.

Blair Cassidy raised her arched eyebrows and gave Maggie a sour look. "Is that how you greet shoppers?"

"You're not a shopper," Maggie said. "You're a manipulative, sneaky, bothersome, bossy—"

Blair held up her hand. "Please, let's not quibble."

"You're right," Maggie said. "Why don't you leave and then we'll get along just fine?"

Blair did not look amused. She heaved a put-upon sigh, as if she were being forced to do something she would rather not. Maggie wondered if Bruce had insisted that she come and apologize. That would certainly be unexpected.

But instead of uttering an "I'm sorry," Blair reached into her purse and pulled out her checkbook, then she wiggled it in the air to get Maggie's attention.

"How much?" she asked.

"Excuse me?" Maggie said.

"How much do you want?" Blair asked. She enunciated every word and spoke very slowly, as if English was Maggie's second, or possibly her third, language.

"Are you buying something?" Maggie asked.

She looked at Blair's arms to see if she'd picked up

something. No, her hands were empty. Was she interested in a piece of furniture? That seemed unlikely, but then would anything that Blair did surprise her? Maybe Bruce told her she had to buy something as a peace offering to Maggie. Unnecessary, but she appreciated the thought.

"Don't be coy," Blair said. "You're a grown woman, a businesswoman; why don't you try acting like it?"

Maggie felt her brain contract as she tried to keep her temper in check.

"I can assure you that I am," Maggie said. "Now what are you talking about?"

Blair slapped her checkbook onto the counter and took out her pen. "How can I make this any plainer? How much do you want to break up with Sam Collins?"

Chapter 9

Maggie shook her head as if she had water in her ears. Surely she must have heard wrong. Was Blair actually offering her money to break up with Sam?

"Are you out of your mind?" Maggie cried. She couldn't help it. She'd had about all she could take of Blair Cassidy and her daughter.

Blair gave her a hard stare, the kind that said she was a woman who always got what she wanted and she wasn't about to start taking no for an answer now. "Everyone has a price. What's yours?"

"Let me be very clear," Maggie said. "You don't have enough money in your checking account to make me break up with Sam."

"Oh, I don't know," Blair said. She glanced around the

shop as if she found it desperately in need of an infusion of cash. "I have an awful lot of money."

Maggie stood and gaped at her. The woman actually thought she could buy Maggie off. She opened her mouth. She closed her mouth. She opened it again. She was utterly speechless, which was amazing, because that pretty much never happened.

"I can see you're struggling with the mental math," Blair said. "How about I get you started with the offer of five thousand dollars? Yes?"

She started to write the amount and Maggie was jolted out of her stupor. What the what? Blair actually thought they had a deal? No!

"No! Stop!" Maggie said. "Absolutely not!"

Blair paused and glanced up at Maggie with one eyebrow raised, as if reconsidering her.

"Summer said you were a savvy negotiator," Blair said. "How about seventy-five hundred?" Maggie saw Mrs. Oliver and her friends approaching with their hats. She smiled at them, trying not to let her ire with Blair show. She didn't want to scare away customers in her attempt to get rid of the crazy woman in front of her.

"No!" she said to Blair through her teeth.

"Fine." Blair's mouth tightened in a look of steely resolve. "Nine thousand dollars, but that's my final offer."

The trio of older ladies looked from Blair to Maggie with interest. Nine thousand dollars was not a number you heard tossed about in St. Stanley.

"No," Maggie said. "And that's my final answer."

"No? To nine thousand dollars?" Mrs. Oliver asked as

she glanced around the shop. "Are you quite sure, dear? What does she want to buy?"

"My boyfriend," Maggie said. She gave Blair a dark, forbidding look.

"Oh, honey, you can have my Gerald for half that," Mrs. Oliver said to Blair.

Blair gave her a disgruntled look. "Thanks, but no. I'm looking for someone a bit more spry."

"He's got a prescription," Mrs. Oliver said with a wink. "It gives him plenty of spry, if you know what I mean."

A snort burst out of Maggie before she could stop it. Mrs. Oliver's friends were chuckling as well, but Blair just looked irritated.

"I can see that this is all just a big joke to you," she said to Maggie. "We'll just see who's laughing when Sam throws you over for Summer."

"Say what?" Mrs. Oliver's friend Patty Trudeau asked. "That's ridiculous. That boy has been following Maggie around for months. It'd take a crowbar and some serious elbow grease to get him off of her."

Maggie smiled at the woman, who had just earned herself fifty percent off.

"Thank you, Mrs. Trudeau," she said. Then she turned to Blair and said, "I think we're done here. Now, good-bye, and I really do mean that from the bottom of my heart."

Blair glanced at her jewel-encrusted watch and heaved a sigh. "Fine. It's just as well. I have a hair appointment anyway. Think about what I'm offering."

She gave Maggie a superior look, stuffed her checkbook back into her purse and sauntered out of the shop. Maggie had the feeling that she had not seen the last of the vile woman. Something had to be done. She simply could not keep dealing with this ridiculousness.

She rang up Mrs. Oliver and company. They had all found hats for their tea and were looking forward to their trip to Dumontville. She was happy for them, but she had a trip of her own in mind.

Grabbing her keys, Maggie retrieved her coat and locked up the shop. She waited for two cars to pass and then hurried across the street to Summer's shop, Second Time Around.

Maggie had never been in Summer's store before. The window display, a full-size cardboard cutout of Summer dressed up in a gaudy cupid outfit, was off-putting to begin with, and she really had less than no interest in seeing what Summer had done with her shop.

The bells jangled on the door as Maggie pulled it open. She stopped in her tracks to take in the scene before her. She felt her mouth slowly slide open, and her power of speech evaporated. Twice in one day—it was definitely her new personal best.

With the walls draped in silk hangings and the scent of incense on the air, Maggie felt as if she'd walked into a scene out of *Arabian Nights*.

"Holy wow," she breathed.

"Can I help—oh, hi, Maggie," Sheri Sokolowski greeted her as she stepped out of the back room.

Sheri was wearing a clingy red jersey dress that hugged her generous curves as if hanging on for dear life. Sheri kept tugging up the front of the dress, which seemed to want to reveal as much of her cleavage as was possible.

Sheri let out an impatient sigh and then grabbed a scarf off a rack nearby and draped it over her shoulders.

"There," she said. Then she smiled at Maggie. "What can I do for you?"

"I was looking for Summer," Maggie said.

"Oh, yeah, Scheherazade is out to lunch," Sheri said drily.

Maggie smiled. "So, I take it you're not loving this?"

"It's a job when jobs are scarce." Sheri sighed. "It would be a bit more bearable if Summer didn't insist on my dressing like a ho, but as I said, jobs are scarce."

"I hear you," Maggie said. "You know, I think Doc Franklin might be looking for a bookkeeper."

"Reaaaaally?" Sheri asked. "I thought Claudia Hughes had a lock on that job."

"She took the secretary job at the high school," Maggie said. "Same hours as her kids and summers off, which is pretty hard to beat."

"Huh, you don't say," Sheri said.

"If Summer asks, no I didn't," Maggie said. "I doubt she'd appreciate my telling you about other opportunities, and I really need to talk to her about her mother."

Sheri rolled her eyes. "Ah, yes, Blair. That woman has been riding me from the moment she arrived in town. I swear if she makes one more crack about my weight, I'm going to sit on her while eating a double scoop, triple brownie hot fudge sundae of which I will savor every bite."

"She does inspire that sort of reaction," Maggie agreed. "Do you know where Summer went to lunch?"

"She said she was stopping at home to grab some things she'd picked up for the shop," Sheri said. "Good luck talking to her about her mother. She thinks that woman is perfect, and is trying to be exactly like her."

Maggie frowned. That was not good news. She'd been hoping that Summer was tired of her mother, too. Oh, well, they still needed to have a conversation about Blair's attempts to buy Sam, and Summer was going to listen whether she wanted to or not.

"Thanks, Sheri, and good luck with the job that I never mentioned," Maggie said.

Sheri grinned and waved to her as she left. Maggie hurried back to her shop to grab her purse. She hated to close in the middle of the day, but honestly, she didn't feel as if she had a choice.

She flipped the store sign to CLOSED and hurried to her car, which was parked down the street. Summer lived on the edge of the center of town in a small bungalow built back in the days when the wire factory was still in business and needed pop-up housing for its workers. The neighborhood had gone from a mid-century utopia for families to a blight on St. Stanley and was now on a surge into artsy housing for unmarried singles and couples who planned to stay that way.

Maggie practiced what she planned to say to Summer the entire ride over. She tried it in her calm and reasonable "let's be adult about this" tone, then she tried it in her angry "I'm going to kick your butt" tone. She preferred the calm and reasonable tone, but she had a feeling angry and butt-kicking was the only thing that was going to get through to Summer.

She parked in front of Summer's house and decided to call Sam. Given Summer's usual histrionics, she didn't want her calling Sam and lying about this visit, saying that Maggie had threatened her or stalked her or whatever.

Sam answered his office line on the second ring. "Sheriff Collins."

"So official," Maggie teased.

"Well, if I'd known it was the prettiest lady in town calling, I would have answered entirely differently," he said.

Maggie felt the same thrill she always did when Sam's voice dropped an octave and whispered in her ear.

"Would you now?" she asked.

"Yes, I would," he said. His voice was almost a growl, and Maggie felt her heart rate kick up as memories of the night before made her blush.

She cleared her throat. "Well, I hate to divert your attention, but this is actually an official call."

"It is? What's up?" he asked. His voice was immediately that of a law enforcement professional.

"I'm at Summer's house," Maggie said. She got out

of her car and walked up the path to Summer's front door.

"Why are you there?" he asked. He sounded confused and concerned.

"Because Summer has to call her mother off," Maggie said.

There was a pause and then Sam asked, "What happened?"

"Blair came into the shop today and tried to buy me off," Maggie said. Her voice was sharp with outrage and she could feel her temper igniting again.

"Beg pardon?" Sam asked. "I think we have a bad connection. I thought you said . . ."

"Yes, you heard me correctly," Maggie interrupted. "She offered me five thousand dollars to dump you so that Summer could have you."

"What?!"

"When I said no, she upped it to seventy-five hundred."

"You said no?" He laughed.

"Yes," Maggie said. "Her final offer was nine thousand, and I said no to that as well."

"I'm flattered," Sam said.

"Because you're worth nine thousand to Blair Cassidy or because I said no?" Maggie asked. She could hear him chuckling, and she supposed it was funny, but she just wasn't there yet.

"Both," he said. This time he laughed out loud.

Maggie sighed and pressed the doorbell. She heard it chime, and she waited.

"Yes, well, anyway," she said. "I've had all I can take

from Blair Cassidy, and I'm going to tell Summer that she needs to muzzle her."

"Uh, do you think that's a good idea, darling?" Sam asked.

"Do you have a better one?" she countered.

She glanced over and saw Summer's car in the drive. She then glanced back at the door. Why wasn't Summer answering? She rang the bell again.

"No, I don't, but you and Summer are like fire and gas," he said. "I'm not sure you should try to have this conversation with her without supervision."

"Oh, it'll be fine," Maggie said. "We're not in high school anymore."

Summer still didn't answer the door. Maggie frowned and tried the doorknob. It was unlocked.

"She's not answering, but her car is here," Maggie said into the phone.

"Maggie, I wouldn't go in there," Sam said. "If she thinks you're an intruder—"

That was all Maggie heard before a scream sounded from the house, making her jump.

"Sam, someone just screamed. I'm going in," she said.

Sam started to protest but Maggie wasn't listening as she pushed open the door and hurried into the house.

"Summer! Summer, are you in here?" she cried.

A mewling sound was coming from the back of the house.

"Maggie! Wait! Maggie, I'm on my way!" Sam's voice was yelling in her ear. Maggie lowered the phone so she could follow the sound of the cries.

She darted through the living room and dining room and turned the corner into the kitchen. She stopped short with a horrified cry.

Summer was standing over her stepfather's supine body, clutching a bloody hammer in her hand.

Chapter 10

"Sam, you need to get here right away," Maggie said into her phone. "And call an ambulance."

"Maggie, what's going on?" Sam cried. He sounded out of breath, and Maggie knew he was probably running for his squad car. "Are you safe? Is there anyone in there with you?"

Maggie glanced around the room. "No, it's just me and Summer and Bruce Cassidy. Sam, I think he's dead."

"What about Summer? Is she okay?" he asked.

Maggie forced herself to look up from Bruce's body to where Summer was standing over him. She was shaking, and her hands had streaks of blood on them.

"Summer, are you hurt?" Maggie asked. "Summer, look at me!"

Summer's blonde hair was hanging over her face. Small whimpering noises were coming out of her mouth. As if she had just registered Maggie's presence, she glanced up and met her gaze.

"Dead," she said. "He's dead."

Summer dropped the hammer onto the floor with a sharp thump and burst into tears. Maggie crossed quickly to her side and checked her over. There were no signs of injury. She put her arm around Summer's shoulder and led her to a stool at the kitchen island.

"As far as I can tell, Summer is shaky but unharmed," Maggie said into the phone. At this, Summer threw her arms around Maggie's neck and began to sob on her shoulder. Maggie patted her back and said, "Hurry, Sam, please hurry."

"On my way," Sam said. "Stay on the line."

Maggie could hear the siren on his car echoing through the phone. From this side of the island, she could only see Bruce's sneakers on the floor. She really needed to check on him, but Summer had her in a stranglehold. Her mind flashed to the pool of blood beneath his head. She really didn't think there was much chance that Bruce Cassidy was still alive.

"Summer, are you sure he's dead?" she asked.

Summer nodded against Maggie's shoulder. Heaving sobs wracked her body, and Maggie patted her back with one hand while keeping the phone to her ear with the other.

Maggie felt as if she were holding her daughter, Laura,

after one of her childhood nightmares. She started to make soothing noises while she rubbed Summer's back.

"It's okay," she said. "I've got you. You're safe now."

Summer shivered against her and Maggie kept up the soothing talk. She couldn't even begin to imagine what must have happened here, but she knew that whatever had happened had shaken Summer to the core.

"Should I get her out of the house?" Maggie asked Sam.

"Does that seem possible?" he asked.

Maggie took that to mean he could hear Summer's sobbing even on his end.

"No," she said. "Not very."

"Look, I'm just down the street, so long as the house seems secure, stay put and stay on the line with me," he said.

"Got it," Maggie said.

She turned her attention back to Summer. Never in a million years would she have thought that she and Summer would be in a situation like this. Still, Summer was hysterical, and Maggie couldn't help but feel sorry for her. It had to have been a shock to come home and find her stepfather like this.

Maggie thought about rounding the corner. Hold on. Summer had been holding the bloody hammer. Had she . . . ?

"Summer," she asked, "was Bruce like this when you got here?"

"Maggie, don't go there," Sam ordered.

Maggie put the phone down. She grabbed Summer by

the shoulders and hauled her away from her. A glance down at her jacket and she could see the wet spots from Summer's tears.

"Summer, look at me," she said. "Was Bruce like this when you got here?"

Summer sniffed. Her long blonde hair hung in her face, but Maggie could see through it. Summer's makeup had run down her face, her skin was blotchy and the end of her nose was red, but she met Maggie's gaze with a tear-filled one of her own.

"Y . . . y . . . yes," she said on a staggered breath. "I came in and he was lying there. I called his name but he didn't answer, so I knelt beside him and he was cold and . . . dead."

Summer paled, then swallowed hard and forced herself to continue, "I kneeled on the hammer, so I picked it up, and that's when you walked in."

Maggie nodded.

"My mo . . . mo . . . mother. I need to call her," Summer said.

"Yeah, we can do that," Maggie said. She picked the phone back up. "Did you hear that?"

"Yes," Sam said. He didn't sound happy. "I'm parking out front right now."

"Sam's here," Maggie said to Summer. She patted her back. "He'll take care of things."

Sure enough, in moments, Sam rounded the corner into the kitchen.

"Hey—" was all he got out before Summer launched herself across the room and into his arms.

"Oh, Sam, I'm so glad you're here," she cried. "I knew you'd come."

Maggie ended the call on her cell phone and tucked it back into her purse. She turned to see Sam hugging Summer. When Summer tried to cling to him, he pulled her off and gently pushed her back.

"Are you all right?" he asked. "Were you harmed?"

"No, not harmed, just—" Summer gestured behind her at Bruce Cassidy's body. "Who would have done this?"

"I don't know . . . yet," Sam said. He pulled a pair of blue rubber gloves out of his pocket and then went to check Bruce out.

Maggie and Summer stayed on their side of the kitchen island. Maggie glanced over, trying to see what he was doing while Summer studied the tips of her high-heeled boots.

Maggie heard Sam call for backup and a medical examiner while they waited. When he came around the granite-topped island, his face was grim. Maggie saw the steely resolve in his eyes and she imagined this was exactly what he had looked like during all those years spent as a detective on the Richmond force.

"I'm going to check the house," Sam said. "I need you to stay right here. Don't touch anything, and don't move."

"Oh no, Sam, don't leave me," Summer cried as she grabbed his arm.

"I'll be right back," he said. He looked at Maggie. "Can you take her?"

Maggie stepped forward and took Summer's arm.

"The sooner he can check the house the sooner he'll be back."

Summer slumped against the counter. They were mostly out of sight of Bruce's body, but to Maggie it loomed like a black cloud on a sunny day. There was no ignoring it.

"I know what you're thinking," Summer said.

Maggie turned and looked at her. "What would that be?"

"That I did it; that I killed him," she said.

"Now why would I think that?" Maggie asked.

"Because you hate me and you think I'm evil," Summer said.

"I don't think you're evil," Maggie lied.

"But you do hate me," Summer persisted.

"Only sometimes," Maggie said. "When you're being, you know, you."

Summer looked as if she was about to start crying all over again, which made Maggie feel like a heel for being honest. Her mother had raised her better than that.

She grabbed a paper towel off the holder by the sink and handed it to Summer.

"Sorry," she said grudgingly. "I didn't mean it. Old habits die hard."

"Apparently," Summer said. "Sorry I threw myself at Sam. Like you said, old habits . . ."

Maggie raised her eyebrows in surprise, and Summer shrugged. They stared at each other and then they glanced away. Things felt abruptly awkward between them. Summer blew her nose while Maggie glanced at the doorway, willing Sam to return.

The ticking of the kitchen clock seemed inordinately loud and Maggie looked around for a distraction.

"What are you doing here, anyway?" Summer asked.

"Oh, I, uh, came to talk to you, actually," Maggie said. "I stopped by your shop, but Sheri said you'd just left to come home and have lunch."

"I was planning to have a salad," Summer said. "I'm trying to lose weight."

Maggie didn't know what to say to that, so she said nothing. Normally, she would tell the person they looked fine, but she and Summer didn't have that sort of relationship. If she said Summer looked fine, it would probably damage the woman's self-esteem beyond repair.

"So, what did you want to talk to me about?" Summer asked. Her voice was strained, as if she was trying very hard to have a normal conversation but it was taking a lot out of her.

Maggie paused. Her original plan had been to rip Summer a new one for sending her mother over to buy Maggie off, but now it just didn't seem important. Bruce was dead. Summer was a wreck. She glanced at the doorway. What could be taking Sam so long? Because there was no way she was engaging in this discussion now.

As if in answer to her silent pleading, a uniformed police officer walked into the kitchen. A petite, sturdy black woman, who more than made up for her lack of height with a feisty attitude, Deputy Dot Wilson glanced from Maggie to Summer to Maggie to Summer again, with her dark brown eyes getting bigger with each twist of her head.

"Sheriff Collins left you two alone?" she asked. "What was he thinking?"

"We're not that bad," Maggie said. Then she glanced at Summer. "Well, I'm not."

"Hey, what's that supposed to mean?" Summer asked. "It's not my fault you have such a hot temper."

Maggie was prevented from answering by Sam reentering the room.

"Everything all right in here?" he asked.

"Fine," Summer and Maggie answered as one. Dot rolled her eyes and added, "Barely."

"Deputy," Sam said as he turned to Dot, "I need you to coordinate a canvass of the neighbors to see if they saw or heard anything. The medical examiner is on his way. Summer, I want you to walk me through everything exactly as you remember it. Maggie, do you mind waiting outside? I want to talk to you next."

"No problem," Maggie said. She was relieved to get out of the house and put some distance between herself and the body.

"You'll be okay waiting here by yourself?" Dot asked as she let Maggie out the front door.

"Yeah, I'm good," Maggie said. She shoved her hands into her coat pockets and leaned against the wooden porch rail while she waited.

A part of her was curious to hear what Summer was telling Sam, but then, another part of her didn't want to know. She had no doubt that Summer was wailing and crying all over Sam at this very minute. On the one hand, she felt sorry for her, but on the other, she knew

Summer well enough to know she was playing the pity card.

It had to have been horrible to find her stepfather like that, but then, if she had just found him, why was she holding the hammer? Maggie felt her heart pound hard in her chest. Could Summer be lying? She wasn't exactly known for having an exclusive relationship with the truth.

But when Maggie thought about it, it had to have been wrenching to find Bruce dead in her home, and Summer had certainly looked to be in a state of shock when Maggie arrived. But was it because Summer had just walked in and discovered the body? Or was it an adrenaline fallout after slamming a hammer into her stepfather's head?

Maggie couldn't imagine why Summer would bludgeon Bruce, but then she wasn't really privy to the inner workings of Summer's life, now was she?

The medical examiner's van pulled up and Maggie opened the front door to let Sam know. "Sam, the ME is here."

"Got it!" he yelled back. In a few minutes, he and Summer appeared.

The blotches on Summer's face had receded. It didn't look as if she'd been crying while talking to Sam. She was still wearing her coat, and Maggie realized they'd both had their coats on the entire time they were inside.

Sam squeezed her arm as he passed by. He stopped by the ME's van and Maggie knew he was apprising him of the situation. The porch was narrow, but Maggie followed Summer to the side where two wrought iron chairs and a short table resided under the overhanging roof.

Summer collapsed into one chair and Maggie sank onto the other. The cold winter air made the cushion crisp and Maggie felt the chill seep through her clothes to her skin.

"Can I get you anything?" Maggie asked.

Summer glanced at her. "No . . . thanks."

With a sigh, she patted her pockets and then frowned.

"Damn it, I must have left my phone inside. I have to call my mother," she said, her tone full of dread.

Maggie didn't blame her a bit.

Chapter 11

Maggie reached into her purse and took out her phone. She handed it to Summer.

"You can use mine," she offered.

Summer gave her an uncomfortable look, as if it pained her to have to borrow something from her. Maggie couldn't fault her for that. If the situation were reversed, she'd feel the same way, but given that Summer had just been blubbering all over her, it seemed ridiculous for them to hang on to the old way of being. Obviously, things had changed, even if it was only for the moment.

Summer tapped in the number and put the phone to her ear.

"It's me, Summer," she said.

Maggie stared off across the yard, pretending not to

listen. She'd get up and move, but there was really no place to go. Instead, she watched as Sam and the ME went back into the house. Sam's face looked grave, and Maggie wondered what he was thinking.

A chill rippled down her spine as she thought of what awaited them inside. Did anyone, even a homicide detective, ever get used to this?

"Well, I'm sorry to interrupt your time under the hair dryer, but it's important," Summer said. She sounded petulant. "Mama, there's a situation. I can't talk about it over the phone. No, you really need to come home now."

Maggie could hear Blair's screechy voice on the other end of the line. She had to give Summer a lot of credit. She would have hung up on her by now.

"We'll talk about it when you get here," Summer said. She was quiet for a minute, then she looked at Maggie. She didn't maintain eye contact, but turned away and hissed, "You did what? When?"

She glanced back at Maggie with an expression that was equal parts mortification and anger.

"I can't believe you did that," Summer said, then she sighed. "It really doesn't matter right now."

Maggie heard Blair protesting. Her argument was clearly not winning points with Summer, because she snapped, "No, it is not okay. You have to butt out. This is my life and I will spend it with whomever I choose."

The squawk on the other end was so loud that Summer jerked the phone from her ear. When Blair wound down, Summer said, "Just get here, and quickly. There's something more important than my love life or your roots."

She ended the call and handed the phone back to Maggie. Maggie tucked the phone away.

"I didn't think I should tell her about Bruce, since she probably wouldn't be able to drive after news like that," Summer said.

"Good call," Maggie said.

"She told me—ugh, she told me she came to see you this morning," Summer said.

Maggie nodded.

"She tried to buy you off?" Summer asked.

Again, Maggie nodded.

"Oh, my god, she thinks everyone has a price just because she does. When is she going to mind her own business?" Summer asked.

Maggie raised her eyebrows. From what she'd seen previously, Summer seemed to be trying to please her mother by going along with her crazy schemes to match her up with Sam.

"Maybe you should have asked her to do that earlier instead of stalking the man she has in mind for you," Maggie said. She noticed her tone was sharp, but she was incapable of curbing it.

"Yeah, about that day at the motel," Summer said. "I was going to warn Sam. I wasn't going to make a play for him. I swear."

"Uh-huh," Maggie said. "Our history makes it hard for me to believe that."

"Fair enough," Summer said. "Tyler said the same thing."

She sounded so gloomy that Maggie couldn't help but

study her more closely. Did Summer Phillips really have feelings for Tyler Fawkes?

"Tyler's not happy?" Maggie asked.

"He dumped me," Summer said. There was no question that Summer was depressed over the breakup.

"But you were just hanging on Sam in there," Maggie said.

"I was upset," Summer said.

"Are you sure you weren't trying to win him over with the helpless woman routine?"

"No, I wasn't," Summer insisted, then she frowned. "Was I?"

"Looked like it to me," Maggie said. "If you want Tyler to take you seriously you have to curb the hanging-on-other-men thing."

"What can I say," Summer said. "It's in my DNA."

Maggie would have argued the point but just then a little black sports car zipped into the driveway and out stepped Blair Cassidy.

Summer stood and waved to her mother, who was looking with annoyance at the ME's van as if it were taking her usual spot without permission.

Maggie stood and Blair's gaze narrowed, as if she thought the reason Summer had called her had something to do with Maggie.

As if preparing for battle, Blair threw back her shoulders and hugged her black wool coat close as if to shield herself from their ire. Then she strode forward as if she fully expected everyone to move aside for her.

Maggie took no pleasure in the bad-news bomb

Summer was about to drop on her mom. How did you tell someone her husband had been bludgeoned to death? She decided she would go wait by her car so as not to intrude upon the scene. She made to leave the porch, but Blair turned on her.

"What are you doing here, Maggie Gerber? Tattling?" Blair asked.

Maggie was forced backward as Blair stomped up the steps, blocking her exit from the narrow porch.

"Um, now might not be the time—" Maggie began, but Blair interrupted.

"I think it's the perfect time," she said.

"No, Mama, it really isn't," Summer said.

Blair gaped at her daughter. "Surely you're not taking her side. How could you? Everything I do, I do for you. Don't you see?"

"There's more going on here," Summer said. She heaved a sigh as if stealing herself for what was ahead. "Come on."

"What? Why? I don't understand," Blair protested.

Summer didn't respond. Instead, she opened the door and led her mother inside. Maggie stayed right where she was on the porch. There was no way she wanted to bear witness to what happened next.

The scream that came from the house made the hair on Maggie's neck stand on end. She hugged her arms about her and thought about the night she had been called to the hospital for her own husband. There was nothing worse than finding out the one you loved was dead.

Restless, she began to pace. Leaves, brown and dry,

littered the small porch and crunched under her feet. No more screams came from the house, for which she was grateful.

The tip of her nose was cold, and her fingers had started to ache from the bitter chill in the air, even with them tucked in the pockets of her coat. When the front door finally opened, it was Sam who stepped out.

He looked haggard, and she didn't hesitate as she crossed the small space to hug him. Sam held her close and rubbed her arms as if he knew the cold was seeping in and he was trying to warm her up.

"Sorry for the wait," he said against her hair. "You'll be able to go soon."

"It's fine," she said. "I know you have a lot going on right now."

"I heard most of what happened while I was on the phone with you," Sam said as he stepped back. "But can you describe to me what you saw?"

Maggie blew out a breath. "The door was unlocked, as I said on the phone, and then I heard a scream. I went inside and followed what sounded like whimpers. When I came around the corner into the kitchen, Summer was standing over Bruce and—"

"And?" Sam asked.

"She was holding a bloody hammer in her hand," Maggie said. She knew what it sounded like, so she quickly added, "I got the feeling she had just picked it up, which is what she said—she said was kneeling on it when she checked on Bruce. It makes sense that she found it."

Sam narrowed his eyes. "Why do you say that?"

"Because she wasn't holding it like you hold a hammer to hit something," Maggie said. "She was holding it with the tips of her fingers like it was something gross that she had found."

"Hmm," Sam muttered. "Then what?"

"She saw me and dropped the hammer and then threw herself at me," Maggie said. "That was pretty much it until you got here. Bruce was clearly dead and Summer was hysterical."

Sam ran a hand over his eyes. "You know, the murder rate in St. Stanley is making me homesick for Richmond."

Maggie gave him a small smile. "It has been a rough few months. You must feel like you retired for nothing."

"Not for nothing."

"Oh?"

"Yeah, there's one thing St. Stanley has that Richmond doesn't," he said.

"What's that?" she asked.

"You," he said. He gave her a quick kiss. "I'm going to have Deputy Wilson take Blair to Doc Franklin's. She screamed and then fainted. The ME thinks she might have concussed herself when she fell."

"No one caught her?"

Sam looked abashed. "We were all caught a bit off guard."

"Doc should probably look at Summer, too," Maggie said. "She was close to hysterical when I found her. I mean, she actually hugged me."

Sam nodded. The front door opened and Deputy Wilson came out with Blair, who was leaning heavily on her, and Summer, who was following behind them.

"We're on our way over to Doc's," Dot said.

"Good. Then I'll need Summer to come to the station," Sam said.

"What? Why?" Summer gasped.

"I'll need a formal statement from you," Sam said. "Since you were the one to find Bruce."

Blair blanched, and Summer looked like she was about to cry again.

"Am I under arrest?" Summer asked. "All I did was find him. I didn't kill him."

"Yes, but you did pick up the murder weapon," Sam said. "We'll need your fingerprints to see which are yours and which belong to the killer."

Blair let out a moan. "My husband. Murdered. I can't bear it."

She slumped against Dot as if she were going to faint again.

"Here, I'll help you get her to the car." Maggie stepped forward and braced Blair on the other side.

When Blair would have pulled away, Dot snapped, "Look, I can't carry you myself, so if you're going to faint, you'd better let her help carry you, otherwise your butt is going to land on the sidewalk."

"Fine," Blair sniffed. She extended her arm for Maggie to take while she helped her to the car.

Summer followed behind them with Sam.

"Are you sure you're not going to arrest me?" Summer

asked. Her voice sounded so scared that Maggie found herself feeling sorry for her—again. It was positively unnerving.

Sam didn't answer her as they navigated the steps and approached Dot's patrol car. Dot opened the back door, and Maggie let go of Blair and stepped out of the way.

"I guess that depends upon you, Summer," Sam said. "And on whether the evidence shows whether you killed Bruce or not."

Chapter 12

Summer wailed and Blair held her close as they huddled in the back of Dot's car.

"Thanks," Dot said to Sam. "Now I'm going to have to run the siren to drown out the crying."

Dot slammed the driver's side door as she got in, and Maggie glanced at Sam. "Were you trying to shake Summer up?"

"Yes," he said. "The fact that she had the hammer in her hand looks pretty bad. Who knows what sort of relationship she had with her stepfather. Maybe he was drunk and made a pass, maybe she actually hated him, or maybe she did just find him like she said. Until the ME gives me more info, Summer is all I've got. So I need her to be nervous so that she'll be very forthcoming with every single thing she can remember."

"I don't think she did it," Maggie said.

Sam looked at her in surprise. "Really? I'd have thought you'd be delighted to see her fingered for murder and carted off to jail."

"Not if she's innocent," Maggie said. "I'm not that heartless. Besides—"

"Besides?" Sam asked when she paused.

Maggie lowered her head and mumbled something into the opening of her coat.

"Sorry, what was that?" he asked. He cupped her chin and lifted her face so that her gaze met his.

"Nothing. It's just that her mother is a horror show and I actually feel sorry for her," Maggie said. "There, I admitted it. Happy now?"

"Yes," he said. He kissed her head. "But I'm not surprised. You have a kind heart, Maggie."

"Maybe," she said. "Hey, I was thinking I'd give Max Button a call, you know, just to let him know that Summer might need his genius legal services."

"Do you think he'd agree to represent her?" Sam asked. "I didn't get the feeling they had the warm fuzzies for each other, since Summer befriended his girlfriend's half sister, Courtney, who is trying to plunder the Madison estate."

"They definitely do not," Maggie agreed. "But even so, Max is trustworthy and a legal genius, so I don't think Summer would refuse his help if he offered. And who knows? Maybe she can call Courtney off of Bianca."

"She'd be crazy if she didn't let him represent her," Sam said.

Maggie grumbled to keep herself from weighing in on the question of Summer's sanity. "I'd better get back to the shop. I can't have people thinking I'm some flighty businesswoman who opens and closes on a whim. It'd kill my business."

"What are your plans for tonight?" Sam asked as he opened her car door for her.

"We're meeting at Joanne's to do a final organization of the nursery," she said.

"No progress there yet?" he asked.

"Not yet. And Joanne is getting antsy," she said. "She's more than ready to meet her sweet pea."

"A baby," Sam said with a shake of his head. He sounded as if he couldn't believe how amazing it was.

Alarm bells starting ringing in Maggie's head. She tried to ignore them, but they were clanging so loud she could hardly think. Did Sam want a baby? This was not the time or place to ask him, but she was beginning to suspect that he did. He seemed so in awe of Joanne and Michael.

Being a guy, Sam was still young enough to easily start a family of his own, but Maggie had been there, done that, and while the idea of a toddler-sized Sam Collins strutting around in a sheriff's hat and diaper had a delicious appeal, she really didn't want to start all over again. She was happy with her shop and her life just as they were.

"I might be tied up late with this," he said. He gestured at the house behind him.

"That's okay," she said. "Call me and let me know how it goes."

"Will do." Sam kissed her quick before she got into her car. "And Maggie, be careful. There's a murderer out there, and I don't think anyone is safe until they're caught and locked up."

"Okay, we've got your small bums here on the left, and then the stack moves on progressively with the baby's size," Ginger said as she backed away from the closet where she'd been sorting and organizing a shelf full of cloth diapers and onesies.

"Whoa, that's a lot of butts to be wiped and changed," Claire said.

Joanne was sitting in the glider in the corner of the room, rocking back and forth as she rubbed her belly. She had a faraway look in her eyes, and Maggie wondered if she was thinking about what it would be like to be holding her baby in her arms at that moment.

"Okay, ladies, snack time for Mama." Michael entered the room, carrying a tray. On it was a pitcher of milk and some glasses, as well as a heaping plate of oatmeal raisin cookies.

They'd had a potluck dinner earlier in the evening, with everyone bringing their favorite dish to share. Maggie loved these evenings because it was a great time to try out new recipes. She'd had the occasional clunker, but tonight's sweet potato casserole had been a keeper.

"I can't eat another bite," Joanne said as she took three cookies. "But the baby sure can."

Michael laughed and leaned over to talk to her belly. "Good baby. We want you big and strong and healthy, so you just take your time, wee one."

Maggie glanced over at her friends and saw that they had identical expressions of "aw" on their faces. She was quite sure she did, too. What was it about a man with a baby that was so attractive?

She thought of how sweet Sam was with her grand-nephew, Josh, and she had to admit, it had certainly been a part of his charm when he'd first come back to town and they were at odds on just about everything else.

"Holler if you need anything," Michael said, and he ducked out of the room after giving Joanne's shoulder an affectionate squeeze.

"You've got a good man there," Ginger said.

"I do," Joanne said. "He's going to be such a wonderful dad."

"Lucky baby," Claire said as she helped herself to a cookie from the plate Michael had left on top of the changing table.

"Thank you," Joanne said.

She looked choked up, and Maggie knew it was because they had tried for so long to have a baby that now that the time had come, Joanne was very emotional.

"Ugh, we have to change the subject," Joanne said. She took a big bite of her cookie, chewed and swallowed. "Let's talk about something else. Any sales happening?

Last I heard, the Millpond Outlets were gearing up for the Presidents' Day sales."

"That is confirmed," Ginger said.

"Michael won't let me go," Joanne said, pouting. "He's worried I'll go into labor and won't give up fifty percent off a pair of shoes to give birth."

Claire laughed. "Well, that's just silly. Now, seventy-five percent, and then there'd be an issue."

Ginger snorted, and they all shared in the laugh.

"I do have some news," Maggie said. She hadn't brought it up before dinner because it seemed bad form, but now that all was quiet and the nursery seemed good to go, she figured they'd all hear it tomorrow anyway.

"Do tell," Ginger said. She sat on the love seat while Claire sat on the floor.

"Our story begins with Blair Cassidy," she said. They all exchanged a look and then glanced back at Maggie. "She came to see me today and offered me nine thousand dollars to stop seeing Sam."

"She didn't!" Claire gasped.

"Wait, wait, wait. You mean a nine with three zeros trailing after it?" Ginger asked, looking stunned.

"What did you say?" Joanne asked.

"Well, naturally, I took the money," Maggie said. "I mean, Sam's nice and all, but really I could do so much more with that influx of cash . . ."

A stuffed teddy bear was launched at her head, and Maggie caught it with a laugh.

"You said no," Joanne said. She grinned. "And I bet you told her off, too."

"Yeah, a little bit," Maggie agreed. "Then I decided to go and have a chat with Summer."

"Oh, now it's getting really good," Ginger said. "What did Summer have to say about her mother?"

"I know what I'd say," Claire chimed in.

"When I went to her shop, Sheri told me she had gone home for lunch, so I drove out to her house to see her," Maggie said. She blew out a breath as she prepared to tell her friends the rest of the story.

"Uh-oh," Ginger said. "Why do I get the feeling this story takes a turn for the worse?"

"When I got to Summer's house the front door was unlocked, so I went inside, and that's when I found Summer standing over her stepfather Bruce Cassidy, who was dead," Maggie said.

"What?"

"No!"

"Oh my god, how awful!"

Her three fellow Good Buy Girls exclaimed at once and then began to fire questions at Maggie so rapidly she could barely keep track of them. She explained that she'd been on the phone with Sam and that he'd arrived minutes after she had. She didn't mention Summer and the hammer, just because she had the feeling Sam would like to keep that quiet.

"Do you think it was a robbery?" Claire asked with a shudder.

"It didn't seem like anything was missing," Maggie said. "I expect Sam will have Summer go through the house to be sure."

"Where will Blair and Summer stay in the meantime?" Ginger asked. "I can't imagine they'll want to stay in Summer's house."

"No idea," Maggie said. "Last I saw they were headed over to Doc Franklin's to be checked out since Blair fainted and sustained a head injury. I called Max and told him about the situation. If Sam arrests Summer, I think Max should represent her."

All three of her friends gave her a doubtful look.

"Would Max do that?" Joanne asked.

"I don't know," Maggie said. "He didn't exactly agree to it."

"Summer has not made a lot of friends in town," Ginger said. "This could be her bad karma at work."

"There is no place lonelier than a jail cell," Claire said. She spoke from experience, having spent some time in jail when she was under suspicion for the murder of a former boyfriend.

"I don't know," Maggie said. "I just don't feel like she did it. And if she gets arrested and she didn't do it, then the real murderer is still out there and we have no idea why Bruce Cassidy was their target."

They were all silent as they pondered this alarming possibility.

"Ow!" Joanne jumped in her chair, and they all turned to look at her. "Sorry, the baby is practicing field goal kicking."

"So it is a boy!" Claire cried.

"Not so fast," Joanne said. "Girls can be field goal kickers, too."

Claire sat back with a frown. "I can't believe we don't know what it is. It's like living in the Dark Ages."

"Buck up," Ginger said. "Judging by how low that baby is hanging, I think it will be out soon."

"Now I'm sort of hoping it waits until after Mr. Cassidy's murderer is caught and St. Stanley is back to normal," Joanne said.

"Yeah, I miss the days when my biggest problem was how to hit two sales at the same time," Ginger said.

Maggie couldn't agree more.

Chapter 13

Maggie was in her shop, looking over her Presidents' Day sale flyers, planning her strategic attack on the stores that day with Ginger and Claire, when she glanced up and noticed that Summer's store across the street wasn't open yet. It was mid-morning on a weekday. The rest of the stores along the town green were open for business.

Maggie couldn't help wondering why Summer's shop wasn't open. Yes, she knew that Summer and her mother were undoubtedly grieving for Bruce, but why wasn't Summer's assistant, Sheri, there? Something seemed off.

She picked up her cell phone and called Sam. He answered on the second ring.

"Sheriff Collins."

"Hi, Sam," she said. "Quick question."

There was a pause, and then he said, "You want to know if I'm still holding Summer as a person of interest, don't you?"

"What makes you think that?" she asked.

"Well, it's mid-morning, and I know Summer hasn't opened her shop as yet, since her assistant Sheri stopped by this morning to give her notice, effective immediately," he said.

Maggie hissed in a breath. "She did?"

"Yeah," he said. His tone was dry. "Something about going to work for Doc Franklin as a bookkeeper."

"Ah," Maggie said. She decided to save the info that she had suggested that job opportunity for another time, like, maybe a year or two down the road.

"So, I'm thinking you probably noticed the shop was closed and were wondering why."

"Impressive bit of reasoning, Sheriff," she said. "So, what's going on?"

"Summer spent the night here," he said. "She is still being held as a person of interest."

Maggie caught her breath. She hadn't really thought that Sam had held Summer overnight. It seemed so severe.

"Are you there, Maggie?" he asked.

"Yes," she said. She wasn't sure of what else to say.

"If it helps, Max is here, and he's talking over her case with her," Sam said.

"That's something, I guess," Maggie said.

"I can honestly say I never thought you and I would have issues with me arresting Summer and you thinking she is innocent," Sam said.

"It is unexpected," Maggie agreed. "Listen, I know that you have your reasons for holding her, but I really can't get over how she looked when I walked in on her yesterday. She did not seem like someone who had just bludgeoned her stepfather to death."

Sam sighed. "I know. I don't like her for it either, but there's no getting around the facts that hers are the only fingerprints on the murder weapon and she was alone with him for long enough to have committed the deed."

"But what about motive?" Maggie asked. "Why would she harm Bruce? What reason could she have?"

"Which is what makes her a person of interest, and not a suspect," Sam said. "I'm keeping her here at the station for a bit longer, but unless I come up with something more solid, she will be released."

"What do we know about Bruce Cassidy?" Maggie asked. "Does he have any enemies?"

"Everyone has enemies," Sam said.

"I don't," Maggie said.

"Really?" he asked. "I could have sworn Summer was your nemesis from the day you punched her in the nose in third grade."

"She stole my Cabbage Patch doll," Maggie protested. "She had it coming."

"And you wonder why I am so surprised by your concern for her," Sam said.

"Believe me, no one is more surprised than I am," Maggie said.

"I'm running a background check on Bruce Cassidy," Sam said. "So far there are no hidden mistresses, gambling debts, alcohol or drug problems looming in his past. Unfortunately, because he is so new to town, I don't have any local dirt on him either."

"Well, someone must know something," Maggie said. "He wasn't here long enough to make any enemies. So, if his killer followed him here, they'd be someone new to town and they'd have to stick out, right?"

"Maggie," Sam growled her name in a low roar that sounded as if he was close to losing his patience.

"Of course, I'm sure you already checked the obvious. Isn't the spouse usually the most likely? I know Blair said she was at the hair salon, but was she really?"

"Maggie, no."

"No what?"

"Do not, I repeat, do not, go digging around in Bruce Cassidy's murder," he said.

"Are you telling me this as my boyfriend or as the town sheriff?" she asked.

"Which one would have the most sway with you?" he asked.

Maggie knew that if she didn't answer wisely, they were going to end up in an argument, and she really didn't want that. The memory of their wonderful Valentine's Day was still fresh in her mind, and she didn't want to ruin it by arguing, especially over Summer Phillips's guilt or lack thereof.

"Well, my boyfriend cooks for me," she said. She made her tone light and teasing. "But the sheriff could arrest me, so I think I will respect his authority, if my boyfriend cooks me dinner."

"I think something can be arranged." Sam's laugh was low and suggestive and made Maggie smile as a thrill went through her. "My place at seven?"

"I'll be there," she said.

She put aside her flyers and spent the afternoon going through the items that she had acquired on consignment. There were three men's suits and a whole slew of dresses from MaryAnn Rigby. She'd been doing Weight Watchers, and every time she went down two dress sizes she donated her old dresses and went on a shopping spree. Maggie was thrilled for her but hoped she stopped before she got so thin that her head seemed too big for her body. That was never a good look.

She had just gotten the items tagged when the front door opened. Maggie glanced up and greeted the man who entered with surprise.

"Well, hey there, Tyler. What brings you here?" she asked.

Tyler Fawkes had not entered My Sister's Closet since he started dating Summer Phillips a few months before and she had forbidden him to step on enemy turf.

He looked sheepish. He took the beat-up John Deere cap off his head and twisted it in his hands.

"Hey, Maggie," he said. "I'm real sorry I haven't been by your shop in a while. It wasn't very neighborly of me, and I feel bad about it."

"It's all good, Tyler," Maggie reassured him. Big and hairy, he lumbered around the small space, making Maggie cringe when he got too close to the breakables. Honestly, it was like having a bear cub in the shop. "I know there were extenuating circumstances that were no fault of yours."

"Yeah, well, about that." He paused and scratched his beard. "I'm here to ask you a favor."

"Me?"

"I'm worried about my girl, Maggie," he said. His voice was solemn. "I need you to help her."

"Say what?" Maggie asked. Shock was too mild a word for the surprise she felt. "Just so we're clear, your girl is Summer, right?"

"Yep," he said.

"The same Summer I just caught you in a motel room with, the same Summer you dumped because she was making a play for my man—you know, the one who has her locked up for murder. The same Summer who has caused me untold years of heartbreak and aggravation," Maggie said. "You want me to help *that* Summer?"

"Yeah, funny, isn't it?" Tyler chuckled as if Maggie were telling a good joke.

"Are you completely out of your mind?" she asked.

Tyler stopped laughing. He slammed his cap back onto his head and a belligerent look took root on his face with the tenacity of crabgrass.

"No," he said. "I know you and Summer have had your issues."

"Issues?" Maggie gasped. "Tyler, in high school she put ketchup packets on my seat in algebra. Do you have any idea how that looked? How mortified I was?"

Tyler started scratching his beard again, and Maggie had a feeling that he was trying not to laugh.

"It's not funny!" Maggie protested. Truly, the more she thought about the history between her and Summer, the more she hoped the other woman rotted in jail. Okay, no she didn't. Especially since she really didn't believe that Summer had anything to do with Bruce's murder.

Tyler must have sensed her wavering, because he looked suddenly serious and said, "Yeah, but didn't she do that because you put hot sauce in her lip gloss?"

Maggie glanced away. "It was self-defense. Besides, Summer started it."

"Maggie, seriously, how old are you?" he asked.

Maggie sighed and flopped down onto the counter, resting her head on her arms. Hadn't she just promised Sam she would butt out? Why was Tyler here now, making a liar out of her?

"Why me, Tyler?" she asked. "Knowing all of the bad blood between Summer and me, why are you asking for my help? I'm not a lawyer or a cop. What can I possibly do to help her?"

"Well, first of all, you're the sheriff's main squeeze, so you have influence."

Maggie shook her head. "I have no influence."

"Whatever," Tyler said, obviously not believing her. "Also, you have a knack for helping people. You helped Bianca Madison when her mother was murdered."

"Yeah, but Bianca was innocent," Maggie said.

"And Summer is, too," he said. "If you ask me, Sam ought to be looking at her mama, that evil woman."

"I can't argue that," Maggie said. "But Blair has a solid

alibi. She was here harassing me, and then she went to the hairdresser's to have her roots touched up."

"Here? She was here?" Tyler asked. "What was she doing here?"

"Trying to pay me not to see Sam anymore," Maggie said. "To open the playing field for her daughter, as it were."

"No way!" Tyler looked outraged.

"Nine thousand dollars of way," Maggie said.

"You didn't take it, did you?"

"No!" Maggie said. "You know me better than that."

"Yeah, but that's a lot of money," he said. "I mean, even true love might waver in the clutches of cold, hard cash."

"So, if Blair offered you nine thousand to stop seeing Summer, would you?"

"Hell no!" he said. "Of course, she didn't need to, because I dumped Summer as soon as I discovered she was listening to that mean old cow and chasing after Sam."

He looked so depressed that Maggie actually felt sorry for him.

"Yes, but she did get frisky with you at that motel, and she told me that she was going to warn Sam about her mother and not make a pass at him," Maggie said. "That has to count for something."

"I s'pose," he said. He sounded like he didn't believe Summer's story to Maggie any more than Maggie had. "Well, listen, this isn't about me and her. I really just want you to do what you can to help her. She didn't kill her stepfather. I know she didn't."

"How do you know?" Maggie asked. She was curious about Tyler's certainty.

"Because I know who she is down in her heart," he said.

Maggie resisted the urge to point out that it was a tiny little raisin of a heart that probably didn't have the capacity to pump out any feelings of love for anyone other than herself. It about killed her, but she kept that observation quiet.

"I know you doubt it, Maggie," Tyler said, correctly reading the expression on her face. "But it's true. My girl has a lot of love to give. She just has to shake her mother off and she'll be fine."

Maggie stared at him for a few seconds. She had promised Sam she wouldn't get involved. But Tyler had come to her; she didn't seek him out. Surely she was upholding her promise if she just conversed with Tyler. Right?

"Okay, tell me what you know about Bruce Cassidy," she said.

"I only met the man briefly," Tyler said.

"Okay, give me your impressions," she said.

"He came across as the indulgent husband and stepfather," Tyler said. "But—"

"Yes?" Maggie prodded.

"Well, before Blair busted us up, I went over to Summer's for dinner, and I watched how they all were, you know, the dynamic between them," he said.

"Really?" Maggie didn't know if she was more impressed by his use of the word dynamic or the fact that he had consciously observed Summer's family. Usually,

Tyler couldn't look past a woman's boobs, so for him to have been on alert and watching dynamics, well, it made her wonder if Summer was even more special for him than he was aware.

"Yeah, and Bruce was tough," he said.

"Tough how?" Maggie asked.

"He made Blair account for all of her spending," he said. "And I didn't get the feeling that it was because they didn't have the money and he was trying to keep a budget, but rather, it seemed like it was a control issue between them."

"Control how?"

"Like he had control over Blair if he had control over her spending," Tyler said. "He liked to come across as all generous, but then he'd say things like 'You'll earn that little bauble later.' "

Maggie frowned. She didn't like that. Frankly, it gave her the creeps.

"How did Blair handle that?" she asked.

"She giggled," he said. "Like it was a game."

"Did it bother Summer?" Maggie asked.

"She wouldn't say, but I got the feeling it made her uncomfortable," he said.

Maggie mulled that over. This was Blair's fifth husband; surely Summer had gotten used to them coming and going in her life. She doubted Summer would feel threatened enough by any of these men to murder them, especially now that she was a grown woman with a business and life of her own. Then again, Blair did seem to hold an awful lot of power over her daughter. If Summer felt her mother was being threatened, how far would she go to protect Blair?

"How uncomfortable?" Maggie asked. "Like awkward uncomfortable, or 'I want to cause you physical harm' uncomfortable?"

"Now hold on there," he said. "I know what you're thinking."

"Really? What am I thinking?" Maggie asked.

"That Summer murdered her stepfather to protect her mother," he said. "And I'm telling you she didn't. I'd stake my life on it."

Chapter 14

"Oh, man, you've got it bad, don't you?" Maggie asked.

"Got what bad?" he asked.

"You're in love with Summer," Maggie said. Tyler's face went slack, as if this had never occurred to him. "Oh, don't tell me this is news to you."

"Well, I mean I like her," he said. He made an hourglass shape in the air with his calloused hands. "I mean, who wouldn't want to drive those curves?"

Maggie squinted at him. Was he for real? How could he be so out of touch with his own feelings?

"Come on, Tyler, dig deep," she said.

"Yeah, well, sure, I care about her," he said.

"Tyler, look at you," Maggie said. "You are here

pleading her case to her archenemy, trying to figure out a way to get her out of being tapped for her stepfather's murder. I hate to break it to you, but you loooooove her."

Tyler flinched. Maggie almost laughed, but he looked so horrified, she couldn't do that to him.

"You need to do some thinking," Maggie said.

Tyler scratched his beard again. He looked perplexed. Given that he wasn't a very deep thinker, Maggie had a feeling that this might take the entire afternoon.

"You're right," he said. He slapped his cap back onto his head. "I gotta go."

He turned and headed to the door. Halfway there, he spun back around. "But you'll think about what I said, right?"

"Yeah, I'll think about it," Maggie said. She was not about to tell him that Sam had all but ordered her to steer clear. She didn't want it to seem like she and Sam had the same kind of relationship as Blair and Bruce. She absolutely did not want anyone, and by "anyone" she meant "Sam," thinking that he could boss her around and she would blindly obey.

The door shut behind Tyler, and Maggie shook her head. She had been doing so well with the butting out until he showed up.

Her cell phone chimed and Maggie picked it up off the counter and checked the caller ID. It was Ginger. Perfect. She needed a girlfriend consultation.

"Hi, Ginger," she said.

"We need to talk," Ginger said.

"Are Roger and the boys all right?" Maggie asked.

"Yes, why do you ask?"

"Because 'we need to talk' generally indicates a big problem, and since I know they're your reason for living I figured it had to do with them."

"It's true, they are, but mercifully, they are all fine," Ginger said. "Summer Phillips, however, is not."

"Oh, no, not you, too," Maggie said.

"What do you mean?" Ginger asked.

"Tyler Fawkes was just in here asking me to look into the situation and to use my influence with Sam to get Summer off," she said.

"Oh, wow," Ginger said. "He's smitten."

"That's what I told him," Maggie said. "I think it was news to him."

"Huh. Why is it men are always the last to realize that they're in love?" Ginger asked. "They're really so thick."

"And Tyler is thicker than most," Maggie said. She laughed. "He left with quite the ponderous look on his face."

Ginger laughed, too. "I can just see it. Sort of like a dog when it hears a high pitched whistle."

"Yup, that's the one," Maggie said.

"Well, listen, you know how I feel about Summer," Ginger said.

"About the same as me," Maggie said. "Only you're less demonstrative in your dislike."

"I never felt the need to show my loathing and contempt in public, no," Ginger said. "Then again, she never made a habit of trying to steal Roger . . ."

"Which would be a game changer," Maggie said.

"Agreed."

"Still, you think we should help her," Maggie said.

"I was just thinking I'd take a peek at the Cassidys' financials," Ginger said. "I'm sure Sam is already on it, but I thought I'd do a little digging, and if I find anything, I'll pass it along."

"Sounds fine to me," Maggie said. "Unfortunately, I had to promise Sam I would keep away from the entire investigation."

"Do tell," Ginger said.

Maggie paced around her shop while she talked, straightening clothes and arranging the furniture. It didn't need it, but she felt a restless energy she had to expel.

"Sam's worried that whoever did this is still out there, and he's concerned that if I butt in, I'll make myself a target," she said.

"Well, it has been known to happen," Ginger said. "He finally got you back in his life—you can't blame the guy for wanting to keep you safe."

"I don't," Maggie said. "I even agreed to mind my own business."

"I hear a 'but' in there," Ginger said.

"He's been away from St. Stanley for a long time," Maggie said. "I know the residents; heck, I even know the passers-through better than he does."

"Agreed," Ginger said. "But if you go back on your word now . . ."

"I know, I know," Maggie said. "It'll damage the relationship."

"Yes, and as you know, good men are hard to come by

in these middle years; they're either taken or, well, they're like Tyler Fawkes, forty going on fourteen."

Maggie shuddered as a picture of Tyler in his underwear streaked through her mind—but not nearly quickly enough.

"Yeah, I know," she said.

"There has to be a middle ground," Ginger said. "You just go about your business, and if people talk to you like I will if I find anything funky, then you tell Sam. He can't get mad at you, because I am doing this on my own and just reporting it back."

"I suppose," Maggie said. "But what do I tell Tyler when he asks if I'm working on the situation?"

"Hopefully, his brain in love is at capacity and he won't ask," Ginger said.

Maggie conceded that this seemed a likely possibility.

"But if he should ask, then you just go all vague politician on him and say, 'Why, yes, Tyler, I am working on it to the best of my ability,' which would be the truth."

"I suppose," Maggie agreed, but she didn't like it. Was being involved with the sheriff going to make her feel this tied down? She wasn't sure she wanted to sign on for that.

As if reading her mind, Ginger said, "Give it time."

"Fine," Maggie said. She knew she sounded pouty, but she couldn't help it. She hung up after Ginger promised to report back with anything she learned.

"Stop thinking about the Cassidys," she chided herself and decided to rearrange the shoe rack at the back of the shop to keep her hands and mind busy.

She had just finished rearranging the shoes and helping Candace Lester unload some of the baby clothes she had sorted from her five growing children when the doors opened and Claire came dashing into the shop.

Candace had picked up two dresses and passed Claire on her way out. She paused to talk to Claire about the waiting list on a book at the library, and Claire gave her a quick nod and blew right past her. Maggie looked at her friend's face and knew immediately that something was up.

"Is Joanne in labor?" she asked. "Are they on their way to the hospital?"

"No," Claire said. "At least I haven't heard anything if they are."

Maggie and Claire both paused to check their phones. No new messages for either of them. "Michael would have texted us," Maggie said.

"For sure," Claire agreed. "I came by about something else."

"A fabulous sale?" Maggie asked hopefully.

"No, why, what have you heard?" Claire asked. She was momentarily diverted by the thought of thrift.

"Nothing," Maggie said. "I am just hoping that you are not going to tell me that you are looking into Bruce Cassidy's murder in order to help Summer. Please tell me you're not."

"Okay, I'm not looking into Bruce Cassidy's murder in order to help Summer," Claire said.

"Thank goodness."

"And now I'm a liar."

Maggie slumped onto one of the two cushy armchairs she had for sale in the shoe area.

"Why are you checking out Bruce?" Maggie asked. "You don't even like Summer. What do you care if she's a person of interest in his murder or not?"

Claire sat on the chair next to Maggie's. "Just because I don't like her doesn't mean she's not one of us. She's the enemy, you know? If she gets locked up, who will be our nemesis then? In great literature, the protagonist is frequently defined by the antagonist."

"I suppose that's one way to look at it," Maggie said. Her tone was doubtful. "Listen, I promised Sam I would stay out of it."

"Good thing I'm here to stick my nose in for you then," Claire said. "I didn't do much, but I did a little digging in the databases at work and online."

"And?" Maggie asked.

"Well, I searched Bruce Cassidy's background in San Diego, California, since that's where he said he was from. I thought if there was a record of any court cases he was involved in, that could show if he left any enemies behind," Claire said. "When I narrowed the search down by age, I discovered there was only one Bruce Cassidy who was a viable match. And that's when it got weird."

Maggie raised her eyebrows. Damn it, now she was curious. "How weird?"

"He was listed as being married to a Sela Cassidy," Claire said. "So, I checked the San Diego Superior Court files to see if there was a divorce on file. There was none."

"Maybe they got divorced somewhere else," Maggie said.

"Perhaps, but didn't he say that he had only just left California and moved to New York when he met Blair?"

"He did," Maggie confirmed.

"So then, why wouldn't the divorce be on file?"

"Maybe she died," Maggie said. "Maybe he's a widower."

"I had the same thought," Claire said. "To prevent against identity theft, they require a notarized application to obtain a death certificate, so the best I could do was search for an obituary. There was none."

Maggie leaned forward. She was intrigued, despite her promise to Sam to mind her own beeswax.

"Do you think he was still married when he married Blair?"

"I don't know," Claire said. "I mean, my databases are pretty limited and specialize in genealogy, and you can only go so far on an out-of-state website, but still, I thought it was pretty interesting that there is no indication of a divorce or a death. Usually those things are pretty easy to trace."

"Sam probably knows this already," Maggie said.

"I'm sure Blair must have told him," Claire agreed.

"Unless she doesn't know," Maggie said.

"Do you think that's possible?" Claire asked.

"From what Tyler described of their relationship, Bruce had all the power," Maggie said. "He was very indulgent with Blair, but he definitely called the shots."

"So he may not have told her about any previous relationships, regardless of how they ended," Claire said. "And Blair doesn't strike me as the type to dig much further than the depth of his pockets."

"Ginger is checking into Bruce's financials," Maggie said.

Claire smiled. "I thought you were butting out."

"For the record, I didn't ask her to look; she called and told me that she was doing it," Maggie said.

"Uh-huh," Claire said.

"Just like I didn't ask you to look into his history," Maggie said.

"You've trained your Good Buy Girls well, sensei," Claire said in a mock-serious voice as she lowered her head in a bow.

"Sam is going to be so mad at me," Maggie said. "But in a town this size, is it really reasonable to think that I could stay completely out of a murder investigation?"

"He won't be mad," Claire said. "He's a very reasonable man."

"I suppose now is as good a time as any to put that theory to the test," Maggie said. "Let's head over to the police station and see if Sam is in. You can tell him what you found out, and maybe Summer can verify whether her stepfather had been married before."

Claire glanced at her watch. "That works. I don't have to be back at the library for forty-five minutes."

Maggie grabbed her purse and flipped the store sign to CLOSED as she and Claire hurried down the sidewalk to the police station.

With each step, Maggie had the feeling she was one step closer to a showdown with Sam. It was not a pleasant thought. Of course, it would have helped if the high noon shoot-out music would stop playing in her head, but she couldn't shake the sensation that if she and Sam did have a showdown, she was going to lose—him.

Chapter 15

"Hi, Dot," Maggie said as they entered the police station and found Deputy Wilson manning the front counter.

"Hi, Maggie, Claire," Dot said. She then hurried around the counter to stare at Claire's shoes. "Where did you get those?"

Claire glanced down at her feet as if she'd forgotten what shoes she was wearing. They were a pair of deep purple suede pumps with gold buckles. "Oh, these old things?"

"Don't you 'these old things' me," Dot chastised her. "I know the latest in Prada when I see it."

"Fine. I bartered for them," Claire said.

"Do tell," Dot encouraged her.

"Aren't you on your lunch hour?" Maggie asked Claire.

"Oh, yeah," Claire said. "Sorry, Dot, no time for shoe talk. I came over to see if Summer wanted any books or magazines while she is . . . er . . . visiting the jail."

Dot looked at her. "Is that a new service the library is offering?"

Claire nodded. "Very new. The idea came to me while I was remembering how long the days were during my own unfortunate incarceration."

Maggie had to glance at her feet lest she give away exactly how new the idea was by grinning.

"Well, that's right nice of you," Dot said.

"Librarians have layers," Claire said.

"So long as one of those layers tells me exactly who and how you bartered for those shoes while we walk back to Summer's cell, it's all good," Dot said.

She led the way to the back with Claire and Maggie following her. Dot noticed Maggie and abruptly stopped with one hand on her hip, "Now just where do you think you're going?"

"To see Summer," Maggie said.

"Why?" Dot asked. "So you can go all 'neener neener neener' on her? Don't you think the girl is suffering enough? Really, Maggie, I thought better of you."

"I wasn't . . ." Maggie began, but Dot cut her off.

"No, you just go sit over by the window where you can't get into any trouble," Dot said. "And watch the phone for me."

"Why?" Maggie pouted. "Is it going somewhere?"

Dot squinted one eye at her and Maggie spun on her

heel and slouched over to the hard bench by the window. She huffed when she sat down, but Dot took no notice of her.

"Now, you were saying about bartering," Dot said to Claire as they disappeared into the back.

Maggie kicked her feet out in front of her. She was pretty sure she had a sulk going on that could only be matched by a two-year-old in the throes of the terribles.

Really, just because she and Summer had scuffed it up before there was no reason to think that Maggie was going to enjoy seeing her locked in a cell. Okay, maybe in the darkest corner of her heart, she might derive a smidgeon of pleasure at seeing Summer suffer, but who could blame her?

The front door to the station opened and Maggie jerked upright. It would not do for Sam to find her there looking sullen. In fact, if it were him, she would be darn lucky she had stayed out front, as in *out of it*. It wasn't Sam who entered, however; it was Blair Cassidy.

Dressed in thigh-high black leather boots, a plaid mini skirt and a puffy red jacket, Blair looked like a tomato with legs. Maggie shook the mean thought aside. The woman's husband had just been murdered. Surely she could find it within herself to be nice.

Blair stopped at the front desk and looked around. Obviously, she was looking for someone to let her in to see Summer.

"Dot just went in back," Maggie said.

Blair swiveled her head in Maggie's direction. She

tossed her black bob out of her face and looked down her nose at Maggie.

"What are you doing here?"

Maggie could tell by her tone that she was looking for a fight. Maggie refused to play.

"I'm waiting for a friend," she said. At least it was the truth.

"So your boyfriend isn't in his office?" Blair asked. "Maybe he is finally doing his job and tracking down my husband's real killer. I registered a complaint with the mayor, you know. Maybe that lit a fire under his backside."

Maggie popped out of her seat. She could feel her temper getting the better of her, and she knew she should keep her mouth shut, but that cow was out of the barn before she could shut the door.

"A murder like this can't be solved in one day," she said. "Oh, then again, it seems to me he has a suspect in custody already."

"Summer did not do this," Blair snapped. "She loved Bruce. She had no reason to harm him."

"Well, someone did," Maggie said. "Who had a beef with him? His last wife? A mistress? A surly relative?"

"No!" Blair stomped her foot. "Bruce didn't have a wife before me, and definitely not a mistress. Why would he need one when he had me? And he had no family other than me and Summer."

"Are you sure about that?" Maggie asked.

"Yes, I am," Blair insisted. "You're just a nasty, vile person trying to make me doubt my beloved Bruce."

Maggie rolled her eyes. "Really? Think about it, Blair. How well did you know him? You were only married for two years. He was in his sixties. He clearly had a long life before you. What makes you think you know everything about him?"

"I just do," she seethed. "Bruce and I didn't have secrets. We had a love someone like you could never understand."

"Actually," a voice interrupted, "Maggie's right. Your husband *was* married before—to a woman named Sela."

Maggie and Blair both turned toward the door. Sam stood there, looking none too happy.

"That's a lie!" Blair said. "You're obviously listening to her vicious gossip instead of doing your job."

Sam pushed his hat back on his head and studied Blair. "Mrs. Cassidy, I understand that you're upset, but I can assure you the information I have comes directly from a standard law enforcement background search on your husband."

"But that's impossible," she said. Her face went visibly pale and Maggie wondered if she was going to faint again. Sam must have thought so, too, because he moved forward so he could be in range if she toppled.

"I'm sorry. I know it must be a shock," Sam said.

"But he told me he had never been married before. You have to be wrong. You have to be!"

"Come into my office, Mrs. Cassidy . . . er . . . Blair, and we can talk about it," Sam said. His tone was gentle, and Maggie felt such admiration for his compassion.

Blair nodded and Sam opened the half door for her that led into the back.

"My office is the first door on the right," he said. "Can I get you water or coffee?"

"Green tea with honey and just a dash of lemon would be lovely," she said.

"Yeah, water or coffee is pretty much what we run on here," Sam said.

"Oh." She looked so distraught that Maggie almost offered to go out and get her tea. "Water will be fine."

"I'll be right in," Sam said. He watched until she disappeared into his office. Then he turned on Maggie. She was pretty sure the look in his eyes was not "hey, I'm glad to see you" but more "oh, man, are you gonna get it."

"Wow, would you look at the time," Maggie said, gesturing at the clock on the wall. "I just popped in to say hi so, uh, hi, and I'd really better get back to the shop. See ya! Call me!"

She was almost home free, and she would have made it, too, if Dot and Claire hadn't appeared right at that exact moment.

"Maggie, wait up," Claire said. Then she noticed Sam standing there looking like a thunderhead about to rumble. "Oh, hi, Sam."

"Hey, boss, what's cooking?" Dot asked.

"My temper," he said.

"Oh, that can't be good," Dot said.

"Deputy Wilson, do me a favor and bring Mrs. Cassidy, who is in my office, a bottle of water?"

Dot glanced at the three of them. "On it. And I will get an explanation later."

She said it as a statement and not a question before she walked back the way she'd come to go to the break room.

"Sit!" Sam barked, pointing to the hard wooden bench by the window.

Both Maggie and Claire sat on the bench. Maggie was studying Sam's face to see how much trouble they were in when Claire elbowed her and bent her head forward, whispering, "Go for repentance."

Maggie mimicked her friend's posture, bowing her head in shame. After a moment, Maggie glanced up to see if it was working. Judging by the tic in Sam's right eye, she was guessing no.

"What were you two thinking?" he asked. His voice was calm, which in many ways was more alarming than if he'd been yelling at them.

Claire looked at Maggie, and Maggie knew she was silently asking how much she should say. Before she and Sam were together, Maggie would have gone with radio silence on what they'd found out about Bruce, but since she and Sam were now a couple, she really had no option but full disclosure.

"Go ahead and tell him what you told me," she said.

Claire's eyes went round behind her rectangular black frames. "Really?"

Maggie nodded. Then she braced herself for Sam's reaction, which she knew was not going to be pleasant.

Claire cleared her throat and told Sam what she'd

discovered about Bruce Cassidy being married before but finding no record of a divorce or death for Sela Cassidy.

Sam paced while she talked, and when she wound down, he stopped in front of them. He craned his head back as if searching the ceiling for patience. Maggie followed the line of his gaze, but unless the old pop-in tiles offered something of which she was unaware, there was no patience to be had overhead.

"This is all information that I uncovered using *proper* police protocol," he said. There was heavy emphasis on the word proper.

"So you already knew Bruce was married before to a woman named Sela?" Claire asked.

"Yes," Sam said. "And that there was no record of a divorce or death for Sela Cassidy."

Claire nudged Maggie with her elbow again. "Wow, he really is good."

"However, I was hoping to interview Blair myself about her husband's past," he said. He frowned at Maggie, who squirmed in her seat.

"Sorry," she said. "She just made me so mad—"

"That excuse doesn't work, Maggie," Sam said.

"It's not an excuse," Maggie protested. If he thought she was going to stand there and listen to someone criticize him, he was seriously mistaken.

"Being chewed out comes with the job," he said. "It's not personal."

"It was personal to me," Maggie said. "I'm sorry, but I am not going to tolerate her insulting you like—"

"You have to," Sam cut her off. "It's going to happen,

especially in cases like this, where a family has been ripped apart."

Maggie knew he was right, but she hated to admit it.

"Now we have a bigger issue here," Sam said. He gave her a dark look. "You promised me, just a few hours ago, no less, that you would steer clear of this investigation."

"Oh, but it wasn't Maggie's fault," Claire said. "She didn't ask me to do any searching. I did it all on my own, and when I told her about it, she insisted that I come here and tell you."

"And when I wasn't here, you just decided to go and visit Summer and fish around about what she knew, is that right?" Sam asked.

"Originally, yes," Claire said. Her cheeks blushed a faint pink with the acknowledgment. "But when I was back there, well, I just couldn't bring myself to ask her about Bruce. She still seems so traumatized."

"Which is why you never should have approached her," Sam said. He turned to Maggie. "And you should have shut Claire down immediately, not come here with her. But did you? No."

"Sam, I'm—" Maggie started, but he interrupted her.

"No, I don't want to hear it," he said. "I'm trying to keep you safe and you're doing your level best to put yourself in harm's way."

"I'm not," Maggie protested. She felt the icky, sticky twist of guilt in her gut. She should have handled this differently. She knew that now.

"Look, I have to get back to Mrs. Cassidy," Sam said. "I think you two should leave."

To Maggie, it felt as if Sam had slammed a door in between them, and she couldn't blame him. She had handled everything wrong. Tyler, Ginger, Claire, all of them. She had promised to butt out, and then she hadn't.

Sam had every reason to be furious with her. When she glanced at him, she didn't see anger, however. She saw cold, implacable resignation, and that scared her far more than any anger he might have shown. She feared this signaled the beginning of the end for her and Sam.

Chapter 16

"Oh, Maggie, I'm so sorry," Claire said as they left the building. "You tried to tell me that you were staying out of it and I completely ignored you and now Sam is mad at you. Gah, I'm a horrible friend."

"No, you're not," Maggie said. "Yes, we probably shouldn't have gone to the jail and no, I really shouldn't have said anything to Blair, but Sam keeps forgetting that this is a small town. People talk. People care about what happens to their fellow residents. He's just going to have to embrace this way of life."

"You sound very pragmatic," Claire said. "But I think that's easier said than done. I mean, he was in Richmond for a long time."

"I know," Maggie said. "Good thing he has me here to help him adjust."

"So you're not upset with me?" Claire asked. She paused as they reached the end of the walkway. She had to go back to the library in the opposite direction than Maggie would take to go back to her shop.

"No way," Maggie said. "You're a Good Buy Girl. I could never be irritated with you unless you scooped me on an amazing sale. Besides, this situation is not your fault. I should have stayed in the shop and had you call Sam and tell him what you found out."

"True, but then I wouldn't have gotten this extensive book order from Summer," Claire said. She pulled out a crumpled piece of paper and glanced at it. "After all my years of being a librarian, people still surprise me with their individual reading tastes."

"Why, what did she ask for?" Maggie asked.

"Not what you'd guess," Claire said.

"No glossy magazines or steamy romance novels?" Maggie asked.

"No. In fact, she wants cookbooks," Claire said.

"Summer cooks?" Maggie asked.

"Apparently, very well," Claire said. "Her preference is for French cookbooks, but she'll take anything gourmet. She says reading recipes relaxes her."

"Okay, yeah, I totally didn't see that coming," Maggie said.

"Call me later," Claire said. "Tell me how things shake out with Sam and, if you get the chance, please apologize to him for me again."

"Will do," Maggie said. She gave Claire, who was not a hugger, a quick squeeze before they set off in different directions.

As she stepped around a few icy patches left over from last night's bitter temperatures, she wondered what she was going to do about Sam. She hoped that once he calmed down, he'd see reason, but she had to admit she didn't really picture it going that way. The big city and a small town were worlds apart, and she and Sam were just going to have to navigate the differences together.

Maggie spent the rest of the day in the shop, trying not to think about Bruce Cassidy's murder, the fact that he had been married before and Blair hadn't known, and that Sam was miffed at her.

Thankfully, she had a flurry of customers who kept her occupied. In the best deal of the day, she sold the two armchairs in the shoe section to a young woman who was furnishing her first apartment. The young woman was a good haggler, but Maggie threw in a lamp and was able to keep the original price.

She was just prepping the shop for closing when her phone chimed. She hoped it was Sam and that their dinner was still on, since it would give them a chance to talk things over. Instead, it was a text from Michael. It declared in all capital letters that Joanne was in labor and they were on their way to the hospital.

Maggie quickly texted Sam that she was going to meet them and would keep him posted, then she dashed out the door. She wondered if Joanne's water had broken or if she was dilated at all.

Her phone kept chirping with texts and she figured it was Ginger and Claire checking in. At the stoplight, she paused to check. Yes, they were on their way. She noted there was nothing from Sam. She hoped this did not mean that he was still annoyed with her.

Maggie parked in the visitor's lot and hurried to the maternity ward. Joanne was already in a room, so she took a seat and waited. She picked up a magazine, but then her attention kept straying to the double doors, where Joanne was, and to her phone, which still had not shown a text from Sam.

It was okay, she reassured herself. He was working a murder case. He was probably tracking down a hot lead and was too busy to text her back right now. This was life with a police officer, and she just had to be patient.

The need to be in motion had her up and moving, and before it was even a conscious thought, she was walking to the front doors of the hospital to wait for Ginger and Claire in the lobby.

She had just reached the first floor when a commotion sounded from the emergency room, which was off to her right. She pushed through the doors with the panicked thought that something had gone wrong with Joanne and she was in the emergency room instead of the maternity ward.

She was halfway into the room when a stretcher with Blair Cassidy on it was wheeled by her. She only got a quick glance, but a medic was moving with the stretcher and holding a pad on Blair's shoulder. Even as they rushed past her, Maggie could see that the gauze was saturated with blood.

Maggie hurried to catch up. "Blair? What happened?"

The medic looked at her. "Are you family?"

"No, but—"

"Maggie?" Blair opened her eyes, looking for her. Maggie hurried to walk along beside her.

"I'm here, Blair," she said. She put her hand on Blair's free hand and the other woman grasped her fingers tight.

"Tell Summer that I love her," Blair pleaded. "I know I wasn't the best mother, but I tried. I really tried."

Maggie whipped her head in the medic's direction and hissed, "How serious is this?"

He glanced between the two of them and apparently decided that holding hands qualified Maggie to ask questions.

"It's a gunshot wound," he said.

"Gunshot?" Maggie squawked.

"I might not make it, Maggie," Blair said. "Promise you'll tell Summer what I said."

Horrified, Maggie said, "Yes, yes, of course."

"And if you could . . ." Blair paused to cough, and Maggie looked to see if she was coughing up blood. No, there was none, but it sounded awful just the same.

"Hang in there, Blair," she said. She felt utterly useless.

"Maggie, if you could . . ." Blair paused to cough again. "If you could see your way to cutting Sam loose so that he can be with his one true love, my daughter, Summer, it would make a dying woman breathe her last breath in peace."

Maggie gaped at her, and then she heard the medic snort.

"You are not dying, Mrs. Cassidy. Far from it," he said. "The bullet just grazed you. It's a flesh wound. A few stitches and some antibiotics and you'll be just fine."

"Is that true?" Maggie asked Blair.

Blair gave the medic a sour look and jerked her hand away from Maggie. "If I do die, you're both going to be sorry."

"No doubt," Maggie agreed, just to be nice. She looked at the bloody gauze on Blair's shoulder and hoped like heck that the medic was right. It seemed like a lot of blood for a grazing. "But I don't understand. How did you get shot?"

"I was checking on Summer's shop," Blair said. "I was just locking up when this truck came out of nowhere. It jumped the curb and the driver got out and shot me!"

How could that have happened across the street from her shop without her knowing? Maggie realized that in her race to the hospital to be with Joanne, she must have just missed it.

"What sort of truck?" Maggie asked. "Did you see the driver? Can you describe them?"

"I don't know. No, I had my back to them," Blair said. She sounded truly rattled, and Maggie didn't blame her one little bit. How terrifying. "It all happened so fast."

"Excuse us, ma'am," the medic said. "We need to get her in there."

"Oh, all right," Maggie said. Then she leaned forward and said, "I'll tell Summer what you said, you know, if I need to."

Blair gave her a wan smile as they wheeled her into a

room where a doctor stood waiting. Maggie turned around to find Sam striding down the hall toward her. She cringed. None of what had just happened was her butting out; in fact, it was very much her butting in. Sam was going to be so mad. Any hope she had of him forgiving her for what happened earlier was about to be blown to smithereens.

"Maggie!" Sam broke into a run. Maggie didn't get a chance to say anything as he scooped her up and held her close. When she leaned back to get a look at his face, he kissed her.

When he pulled away, she was left breathless and weak-kneed while he ran his hands all over her as if to reassure himself that she was in one piece.

"Oh, man, I think I just had four heart attacks. I heard the call on the radio that there had been a shooting in front of one of the consignment shops in town," he said. He cupped her face. "You're okay? You're really okay?"

"I'm fine," Maggie said. Then he kissed her again. She hugged him close. This was infinitely better than him being miffed at her.

"Sam, it wasn't my shop," she said. "It was Summer's. Blair was locking up and a truck jumped the curb and stopped in front of her and the driver got out and shot her."

"How is she?" he asked.

"The medic said the bullet just grazed her and that she'll be okay."

Sam frowned, and she could tell he was thinking it over, sifting through the facts in his cop brain.

"I promised Blair that I'd go and tell Summer that she

loves her," Maggie said. Sam opened his mouth to speak but Maggie held up her hand. "I know you want me to butt out, but honestly, in a town this small, it's virtually impossible. That being said, when I made that promise to you I did mean it. I just didn't know how hard it would be to keep it."

"It's okay," Sam said. "Deputy Wilson pointed out to me, in her usual subtle way, the impossibility of my request. Although she did say it was impossible because you're terminally nosy."

"She did not!" Maggie protested.

"Yes, she did," he said with a laugh. "Now don't get your nose out of joint over it."

"Hardy har har," Maggie said. She was so relieved that things were good between them, she didn't mind the teasing. In fact, it made her feel as if they were a-okay.

"So how did you find out about Blair?" Sam asked.

"I was here because Joanne—oh my god, Joanne!" Maggie cried, and then she turned and began to jog out of the ER. "She's having the baby!"

Sam watched her go with a grin. "I'll be up as soon as I can."

"I'll text you if there's news," Maggie said.

Then she blew him a kiss and bolted back up to the maternity ward. She was just rounding the corner when she slammed into Ginger, who was pacing. She almost knocked her down but Claire leapt forward and caught her.

"Sorry!" Maggie cried.

"Where have you been?" Claire asked.

"We thought you were already here, and then we heard

sirens," Ginger added. "Lord-a-mercy, we had you dead in a car accident."

"I'm sorry. I was here, but I was down in the ER," Maggie said. "While I was waiting for you, Blair Cassidy was brought in. She's been shot!"

"No!" Claire and Ginger gasped together.

"Yes," Maggie said. "She was checking on Summer's shop, and when she was leaving, a truck hopped the curb in front of her and the driver got out and shot her. Then they sped off."

"Did she see who it was?"

"No, she seemed fuzzy on the details. But I'm sure Sam will help her remember more."

"First Bruce, now Blair—who do you suppose has it in for the two of them?" Claire asked. "Maybe they were bank robbers like Bonnie and Clyde and now the law is coming to get them."

"No, the law doesn't hop out of a truck, shoot you and take off," Ginger said. "This is personal."

"I don't know why," Maggie said. "But whoever it is, they seem willing to go to any extreme to get the Cassidys."

Ginger shuddered. "I'm not overly fond of Blair, but I can't help but feel sorry for her. I can't even imagine how terrified she must be."

Maggie gave a wry glance. "Not terrified enough to miss the opportunity to ask me to dump Sam as a mother's dying wish."

"She. Did. Not," Ginger said.

"Oh yes, she did," Maggie said. "I almost fell for it, too, but the medic told me she was going to be fine, so I made no promises that I'd have to break."

"Wow. Bruce did say she was a terrier when she made up her mind that she wanted something," Ginger said.

"I'd say 'terror' is more like it," Claire said.

The doors that led to the maternity ward opened and Michael and Joanne walked out. Maggie could tell by the look on Joanne's face that her hopes to meet her baby had been dashed once more.

"False labor again?" she asked.

Joanne didn't say anything. She opened her mouth to speak, but the only thing that came out was a weepy wail as she started to cry.

"I am so tired of being this big beached whale who can't tie her own shoes and never sleeps," she said in a sob-studded stammer that the others had to strain to decipher.

As one, the Good Buy Girls formed a huddle around her, patting her back and hugging her. Michael stood awkwardly and charmingly in the thick of it, never leaving his wife's side.

"So is this what you four do right before you hit a sale?" he asked. "Huddle up?"

"Hush!" Ginger shushed him. "You're here in a support capacity only."

"Okay," Michael agreed, and clamped his mouth shut.

"Now think of this pragmatically," Claire said. "The closer you are to your due date when you deliver, the stronger your baby will be."

"And," Ginger chimed, "when the time comes, you get the awesome push diet."

Joanne sniffed. "Push diet?"

"Yeah, you push that baby out and you lose an immediate twelve pounds," she said. "And the bigger the baby is, the bigger the weight loss for you."

Joanne chuckled while she wiped the tears from her eyes.

"And the baby will have built up all of its immunity," Maggie said. "Which will be excellent timing given that we're on the tail end of the flu season."

"You're right. I know you're right," Joanne sniffed. "I just feel like such a boob. I swear I really thought it was the real deal this time."

"Not your fault," Claire said.

"Yeah, the baby is probably giving you a few practice runs so that by the time it is really happening, you'll be all, 'No big deal,'" Ginger said.

This time Michael laughed. "That baby has our number."

The huddle broke up as the rest of them started laughing. Michael hugged Joanne close and said, "Come on, let's get you home so you can try to get some sleep."

"I'll walk you out," Ginger said.

"Me, too," Claire said.

They looked at Maggie and she said, "I think Sam is still in the building. I'm going to try and find him."

She gave Claire and Ginger a meaningful look and then looked at Joanne. She didn't think Joanne needed to hear about people being gunned down on the street. She had enough on her mind as it was. They both nodded. At the main floor, Maggie left them to go back to the ER.

She was just pushing through the swinging doors when she saw Dot entering from the other side with Summer Phillips beside her.

"You!" Summer cried when she saw Maggie. "What did you do to my mother?"

Chapter 17

Maggie looked at Dot. "She did not just say that, did she?"

"She's a little distraught," Dot said.

"My mother has been shot!" Summer cried. "I am more than distraught."

"Summer, I am sorry about your mother, but when I spoke to her—" Maggie began, but Summer interrupted.

"You spoke to her? When?"

"Just a short while ago," Maggie said. "She asked me to tell you that she loves you and that she knows she wasn't the best mother but she tried."

"Oh, my god," Summer cried. "She's dying, isn't she?"

"No, she isn't," Dot said. "We would have had you over here a lot earlier if the situation were critical. Your mother will be fine."

Dot gave Maggie a reproving look. Maggie shrugged and said, "I'm just telling her what Blair told me to say. It's not my fault she was feeling dramatic."

"And it didn't occur to you to filter it? Shoot, from what you just said, even I thought she was dying, and I know better," Dot said.

"Sorry," Maggie said. "I wasn't thinking. I was here because Joanne was in labor—"

"Did she have the baby?" Dot asked. She looked so excited that Maggie hated to dash her hopes.

"False labor," Maggie said.

"Aw, man," Dot said. "Again?"

"Hello? People? My mother!" Summer said.

"Oh, yeah, come on," Dot said. "Sheriff Collins told us to meet him in room 132."

Maggie started to walk with them, and Summer scowled at her. "Why are you coming along?"

"To see Sam," she said.

"Oh, yeah, that's right," Summer sneered. "You're in looove."

Somehow she managed to make it sound cheap and tawdry, as if Summer had any call to criticize her relationship. Maggie felt her temper beginning to heat.

"Says the woman who was found in a motel with Tyler Fawkes in his underwear," Maggie scoffed.

Summer whirled on her, her bleached-blonde, extension-enhanced hair flying. "Don't you say anything bad about Tyler!"

"It wasn't Tyler I was insulting," Maggie said. She gave Summer a pointed look.

"Why, you—" Summer's hands extended like claws and Dot had to hold her back before she sank them into Maggie's face.

"Will you two quit it!" Dot snapped. "Good grief, you'd think you were still in kindergarten. Wait, I take that back. That's an insult to five-year-olds, as they certainly behave better than you do. Now let's go."

Maggie moved to walk on the other side of Dot so that she wasn't in clawing range of Summer. She felt badly about tiffing with the other woman. Summer had been having a rough couple of days and Maggie should be more understanding, but oh, that woman could get under her skin faster than a tick on a dog's ear.

When they reached the room where Blair was being treated, Sam was standing by the door. He looked surprised to see Maggie with Dot and Summer, and his eyebrows lifted in question.

"False labor," she said.

He gave a pained look as if he knew that it hadn't been received well by the parents. Maggie shrugged, and he nodded.

"How is my mother?" Summer asked. "Is she . . . is she dying?"

"No!" Sam said. His reaction was so strong that Maggie suspected he'd been getting quite an earful from Blair. "I think the doctor will let you in to see her now. In fact, I could use your help in getting her to talk to me about what happened."

Summer gave him a quick nod and started toward the door.

"I'll wait right here," Dot said. "Remember, I'm your ride home."

From the way she said it, it was clear to everyone that "home" meant "jail."

Maggie stood beside Dot while Sam and Summer went in to see Blair. A nurse came out while they waited, and Dot took the opportunity to wedge her heel in the door, leaving just enough of a gap so that they could hear what was being said.

"You are sneaky," Maggie said.

"Shh," Dot hushed her. "The preferred terminology is 'innovative.'"

"Mama, are you all right?" Summer asked. "Where were you shot? What did the doctor say? Are you in a lot of pain?"

"Summer! Thank goodness you're here. Oh, and look at the two of you," Blair cried. Her voice was slurred, as if she'd had a martini or two, which made Maggie think they'd loaded her up on pain meds. "It makes a mama's heart full to bursting to see her baby with the man of her dreams."

Maggie exchanged a glance with Dot, who put up her hand as if to say, "Wait for it."

"Mama, Sam is not the man of my dreams," Summer said. "And you really need not to be thinking of my love life when you were very nearly murdered."

"Blair, I need you to tell me everything you remember from right before you were shot," Sam said in his most officious sheriff voice.

"Oh, dear Sam, look how intent he is upon finding the

person who harmed his lady love's mother," Blair said. "You should hang on to him, Summer. He's a keeper."

"Mother!" Summer sounded as if she was finally at her wits' end. "Sam is not mine to hang on to."

"Of course he is, dear," Blair said. "Just look at the two of you. You make such a lovely couple—not like you and that knuckle-dragger Tyler Fawkes. Honestly, what were you thinking shacking up with him?"

Maggie couldn't stand it. She had to peek. Sam was standing on one side of the bed and Summer on the other. Sam looked irked, Summer had her eyes shut as if praying for patience, while Blair swiveled her head between them, looking delighted.

"Ladies, could we please stay focused on what happened tonight?" Sam asked. "Blair, about the truck that stopped in front of the shop—what do you remember?"

"It was a dark-colored vehicle," she said. "It was clearly not an import; just big and clunky, nothing worth noticing."

"Yeah, except that your shooter was driving it," he said. "So, anything you can remember, anything at all, would be really helpful."

"Tyler is not a knuckle-dragger!" Summer burst out as if completely unaware that they had already changed the topic. "He is a good, kind man, and any woman would be lucky to have him."

"Uh-oh, them's fightin' words," Dot said. She squeezed in under Maggie to get a glimpse of the action through the crack in the door.

"Now you listen to me, Summer Phillips," Blair said. If she was feeling weak from blood loss or woozy from meds, it did not show. "I did not raise you to settle for some no-account, minimum-wage-earning loser. What does that man even do?"

Summer opened her mouth to respond, but Blair never gave her the chance as she continued her tirade.

"You are a beautiful young woman who was bred to find a man who can care for you and provide for you in the manner to which you should become accustomed."

"No!" Summer snapped. "That's enough, Mama. I care for Tyler Fawkes. No, he may not be incredibly attractive or have a lot of money, but he makes me feel special and he makes me a better person, and I—well, I love him!"

The room went silent for the space of a heartbeat, and then Blair went apoplectic.

"Nurse!" Blair cried. "I need a nurse!"

Summer and Sam scrambled around looking for the call button. They were too late.

A woman in pale blue scrubs came rushing into the room from a door that connected to the next room. She was hobbling, favoring her right leg as if she'd hurt the left one in her hurry to get to Blair. She had her hair tucked into a surgical cap, and a mask covered her lower face. She moved it aside as she asked, "What is it, Mrs. Cassidy?"

"The pain, oh, the pain," Blair cried. She clutched her chest.

"Is it your wound?" the nurse asked. She frowned. She did not appear overly sympathetic, and Maggie couldn't blame her if she'd injured herself on her way here only to find Blair in the middle of a dramatic episode. "Your pain medication should have kicked in by now."

"No, it's not my *gunshot* wound, it's my heart," Blair said. "It's breaking."

"Oh my god," Summer said. "I need a drink."

"There's a water fountain in the hall," the nurse said.

"Well, unless it's spitting vodka, it's of no use to me," Summer snapped.

"We need to take your mother up to her room," the nurse said.

Sam had finally located the call button. While putting it on the bed, he accidentally pressed the button.

"What are you doing?" the nurse barked at him.

"Sorry," Sam said, and raised his hands in the air as if she had a gun on him.

The nurse glared at Sam and Summer. "You can come back tomorrow."

"I'll be dead by then," Blair said.

"Mama," Summer whined.

Another nurse passed Maggie and Dot as she joined the group in the small room. "Is everything all right in here?"

"Yeah, thumbs here hit the button by mistake," the first nurse said, gesturing toward Sam.

The other nurse nodded and then glanced around the room. "It's just as well. Your room upstairs is ready, Mrs. Cassidy, so I'll take you up now."

"I can take her," the first nurse said.

"I'm on rotation up there. It's fine," the second nurse said.

She began to prep Blair's bed while Summer stepped close to hug her mother good-bye. Blair refused to hug her back.

"I'll be posting a detail outside your door, Blair," Sam said. "We'll be keeping a close eye on you until the shooter is caught."

Blair heaved a deep sigh. "At least *someone* cares." Then she rolled over on her good side, facing away from Summer.

The nurse began to wheel Blair out of the room, and Sam gestured for Summer to come with him.

"Good night, Mama," Summer said.

Blair did not respond. It was then, as Maggie watched Summer's face crumple with guilt and remorse, that she finally understood what Bruce had told her before about Summer's life. Summer had been expected to be the prettiest and snag the richest boyfriend or husband, and suffered guilt-laced silence if she didn't. She couldn't help but feel sorry for her.

"Scooch," Dot said, pulling Maggie aside as Summer and Sam pushed through the door.

"Deputy Wilson, I'll take Summer back to the station if you'll take the first shift watching over Mrs. Cassidy," he said.

"Yes, sir," Dot said. "Don't you worry, Summer. I'll keep her safe."

"Thanks, Dot," Summer said. Then she threw herself into the smaller woman's arms and gave her a crushing hug.

Maggie could tell Dot was taken aback, as her eyes went wide and it was a moment before she returned the hug with an awkward pat on the back.

As Dot followed the stretcher that carried Blair Cassidy down the hall, Sam walked Summer and Maggie out. They paused by Maggie's car, where Sam gave her a quick kiss and said, "I'll call you later."

"We can order a pizza," Maggie suggested.

"Fully loaded?" he asked, and she nodded with a smile.

"You two make a cute couple," Summer said. "Sickening, but cute."

"Thanks, I think," Maggie said. She wasn't sure what to make of Summer like this. Then again, she wasn't sure what to think about Summer's declaration of love for Tyler. She wondered if Tyler knew.

Yeah, she knew it was none of her business, but still, the romantic side of her refused to let Summer's mother destroy whatever might be happening between Summer and Tyler. And wouldn't Sam be happy that she was butting out of murder and butting in to romance?

She waved to them as she drove off, wondering how she was going to engineer a meeting between Tyler and Summer with Summer still behind bars. There simply had to be a way.

Chapter 18

"This is quite possibly the stupidest idea you've ever had," Ginger said.

"Don't be such a doubter," Maggie said. "Tyler needs to know how Summer feels about him before Blair poisons Summer any further. And if he visits her in the jail, she'll see that he cares, too."

"And you think that you can get him to go to the jail with you because—?" Ginger asked.

"I need his truck," Maggie said. "I put in a bid on two of those vintage steel desks, you know, the sort built to survive a nuclear attack, that they auctioned last month and I just got the notice that I won. Tyler picks up stuff for me all the time, so this is perfect."

"How is it that he is going to see Summer when she's in lockup?"

"It could be that she's getting released about the same time that we're picking up the desks," Maggie said. "I'm awaiting a text from Dot to coordinate our efforts."

"So, Summer is off the hook?" Ginger asked. "Sam doesn't think she killed her stepfather?"

"Well, since her mother was shot while she was locked up, it does seem unlikely that she had anything to do with Bruce's murder, if the two are connected, which Sam seems to think they are," Maggie said. "Plus, I think they had to either charge her or release her, and I don't think Sam was ready to charge her. She just didn't have a motive to kill Bruce."

The bells on the door chimed and Tyler poked his head in.

"Maggie, you ready to roll out?" he called. "I promised Tim Kelly I'd help him move this morning."

"Just let me grab my purse," she said. She hurried into the back room and grabbed it from her desk. "Thanks for watching the shop for me, Ginger. I promised myself I wouldn't close again in the middle of the day. I swear I won't be long."

Ginger just shook her head at her friend. "I still say you're crazy. But good luck!"

Maggie grinned and let the door swing shut behind her.

Tyler's well-loved pickup truck was parked curbside in front of the shop. He opened the passenger door for her and Maggie climbed up and in, noting that the pine-shaped air freshener hanging off the rearview mirror was working triple overtime. She was pretty sure she felt her nose hair curling in response to its overpowering fake piney scent.

"So, what are we hauling today, Maggie?" he asked.

"A couple of desks; heavy steel ones. Did you bring the ramp and handcart?"

"Of course," he said. "Where are the desks?"

"Head toward the center of town," she said. "I'll talk you through the directions."

Tyler shifted the truck into drive, using the lever on the right side of his steering wheel. He waited until the road was clear and then he made a wide U-turn to take them to the center of town. Maggie waited until they were right in front of the police station.

"You want to park, oh, right about here," Maggie said.

"What?" Tyler squawked. "Give a guy a little notice, Maggie."

"Sorry," she said. Little did he know she was apologizing for a lot more than poor directions.

Tyler braked hard and eased the truck up against the curb. He maneuvered it in between two parked cars, parallel parking like a pro. Once he shut off the engine, Maggie hopped out of the truck and gestured for him to follow.

"Come on," she said.

He didn't move. He sat staring at the red brick building behind Maggie, plucking his lower lip between his thumb and index finger.

He leaned across the seat, looking at Maggie through the open passenger door. "I'll wait here."

"You can't!" Maggie protested. "I need you to help me figure out logistics and stuff. Those desks are really big and awkward and I need your expertise."

Tyler frowned at her. "Maggie Gerber, I've known you my whole life. You are the worst liar ever. I was there when you tried to tell our third-grade teacher, Mrs. Campbell, that the dog ate your homework."

"It was a good excuse," she protested.

"Oldest fib in the book and hampered by the fact that you did not have a dog, which Mrs. Campbell knew. Besides you have an inability to maintain eye contact when you lie," he said. "It's a dead giveaway."

"I can, too," Maggie argued. She stared at him as hard as she could, bugging her eyes out.

"So, why are we here?" he asked.

"To pick up those desks," she said.

"Ha! You just looked away!"

"I did not!"

"Did, too," he said. "Maggie Gerber, what are you up to?"

"Nothing," she squeaked. This time she felt her eyes dart away. Darn it, why was she such a bad liar?

"Maggie, what would your mama say if she saw you right now?" he demanded. "Telling whoppers and not even being the least little bit ashamed."

"I'll tell you what my mama would say," Maggie snapped, getting irritated by Tyler's stubbornness. "She'd say, 'Why isn't that Tyler Fawkes getting out of his truck to help my baby girl like a proper gentleman should?'"

Tyler heaved a sigh. "I can't go in there, Maggie. *She's* in there!"

"*She* as in Summer?" Maggie asked. "Well, I have some news about that, but I'm not sure I'm going to tell you now, since you're being such a big chicken."

"News? What news?" he asked.

"Come on," she said. "I'll tell you on the way."

"Is it good news?" Tyler asked cautiously.

"Very," Maggie said. Then she slammed the door and began to walk toward the station, leaving Tyler to race after her. She checked her phone to make sure they were still on schedule. Yes, Dot's text said they were processing the paperwork right now.

"So what is it?" he asked. "And no more lies."

They were almost to the doors when Maggie turned to him and said, "I heard Summer tell her mother that she loves you."

This time she maintained eye contact and put her hand over her heart to add a measure of veracity to her statement.

Tyler's eyes popped wide open and he went slack-jawed, then he shoved her shoulder and said, "Shut up!"

He squealed like a teenage girl, and it was all Maggie could do not to laugh. She might have if his shove hadn't smarted so much.

"Ow," she said, rubbing her shoulder.

"Sorry." He looked contrite, and then suspicious. "Are you messing with me, Maggie? 'Cause that would just be mean."

"Am I known for being mean?" she asked.

"Well, according to Summer—" he began, but she interrupted.

"To you," she clarified. "In all of the years that you've known me, have I ever been mean to you?"

"Well, no," he said.

"Then trust me," she said. "She went toe to toe with her mother for you. Now you need to show her some support or she's going to get over you so fast you'll hiccup and she'll be gone."

Tyler gasped and then yanked open the door and strode into the station. He stopped in the lobby, standing with his hands on his hips, looking like Superman surveying the scene before him.

Maggie, unprepared for him to stop short, plowed into his back. She bounced off, as Tyler didn't move. Wondering what had him rooted to the spot, Maggie glanced around him to see Dot and Sam standing at the front desk with Summer.

Summer and Tyler stared at each other, but no one spoke. Maggie dug her knuckle into Tyler's back to propel him forward—hopefully with his verbal skills fully functional.

"Oh, uh, hi, Summer," he said as he moved away from Maggie.

Maggie sighed, as her hopes for his verbal functionality were obviously for naught.

"Hi, Tyler," Summer said. She fiddled with the ends of her hair and glanced down at the paperwork in front of her as if embarrassed.

Maggie had to give Dot credit. She had obviously overseen Summer's wardrobe choices for the day. Who knew the deputy had such skills in the makeover arts?

Summer was in a long, flowing floral dress with cute ankle boots and a denim jacket. Her blonde hair was done in careless waves down her back, and her makeup was much lighter than usual. She was the picture of a sweet damsel in distress.

Since Tyler had always seemed partial to the overly madeup, sexy Summer, Maggie wasn't sure this was the best outfit choice, however much she liked it herself, but one look at Tyler's dumbstruck face and she knew Dot had been spot-on.

She glanced at the deputy with her eyebrows raised, and Dot winked at her.

"Just one more signature," Sam said. "And then you are free to go—just don't leave town."

"Do you need a ride?" Tyler asked. "I've got my truck right outside, and I'd be happy to give you a lift anywhere you need to go."

And just like that, Maggie knew she had been thrown over. She would have been irritated if this hadn't been a part of her plan all along.

"Oh, I have a ride," Summer said. "But thank you. That's very sweet of you, Tyler."

Summer rested her hand on Tyler's forearm and gazed up at him through her lashes. Maggie was surprised he didn't drop to one knee and pop out a proposal right there, but she had a feeling his brain matter had turned to mush, making his motor skills all but useless.

She shot a glance at Dot, who shrugged. Obviously, she had no idea who Summer's ride was either.

"You know I'd do anything for you, don't you?" Tyler

asked Summer. His voice was so tender, Maggie felt her own throat get tight as she watched the two of them.

Summer blinked at him and blushed a faint shade of pink. "You are so wonder—"

"That's it!" a voice cried from the front door.

They all turned as one to see Blair Cassidy entering the station with her arm in a sling and a uniformed driver holding the door for her.

Sam came out from behind the desk as if he anticipated trouble. He moved to stand beside Maggie, and out of the corner of his mouth, he asked, "What are you up to, darlin'?"

"Me?" Maggie asked. She tried to bite her lip and look at him through her lashes like Summer had done to Tyler, but judging by the grin he seemed to be unsuccessfully fighting off, she did not have the same stupefying effect.

"What's 'it,' Mama?" Summer asked. She glanced nervously at Tyler, as if afraid he was the answer to her question.

Maggie wondered if Summer would take on her mother again in defense of Tyler. If she did, Maggie suspected this could get downright ugly.

"The truck that jumped the curb when I got shot!" Blair cried. She turned to Sam. "Did you catch him? Is that why it's parked out there?"

Sam blinked. "What are you talking about?"

Blair marched back to the glass doors. Her driver jumped out of the way before she stomped over him. She tapped one of the glass panes with a well-manicured red fingernail.

"That's the truck, the one parked right there, that was driven by the person who tried to shoot me," she said. "I'm sure of it."

As one, they all crowded toward the doors to look.

Tyler was the first to speak. "But that's my truck."

Blair sucked in a breath and scurried around her driver as if using him as a human shield. The poor guy had no idea what was going on, and flinched when she gripped his upper arm with her good hand and dug her nails in. The man couldn't escape if he tried.

"So, it was you!" Blair cried, glaring at Tyler. "You tried to kill me!"

Chapter 19

"What? No!" Tyler protested. "I would never!"

"Don't you lie to me!" Blair screeched. She lifted up her arm in the sling. "Look what you did to me."

"Mama, if he says he didn't do it, he didn't do it," Summer protested.

"You get away from him," Blair said. She reached around her driver and grabbed Summer by the arm, yanking her close. "He tried to kill me. He could try to kill you, too."

"No, I didn't!" Tyler argued. He fisted his hands in his hair, looking as if he might rip it out by the roots.

"Blair, this is a serious accusation. Are you absolutely certain that is the truck?" Sam asked.

"Yes," Blair said.

"I thought you said your back was to it and you didn't see anything," Maggie said. She didn't doubt for one second that Blair would use this as an opportunity to break Tyler and Summer up.

"I was turned away, but I knew it was a truck because I saw its reflection in the window," she said. "And I remember that streak of bright green paint on the front bumper. It was the last thing I saw before I was shot!"

"That is distinctive," Dot said. "A streak of lime green like that will stick in the brain. How'd that happen, anyway?"

"I was doing some painting over at Mrs. Tibbets's day care center," Tyler said. "One of the little crumb crunchers decided to paint my truck green. Luckily, I caught him before he moved on from the bumper."

"Oh, yeah, that could have cost you," Sam agreed.

"A splash of paint doesn't prove anything," Summer said to her mother. "I'm sure a lot of trucks have splatters of paint on them."

"In that shade of green?" Blair asked.

No one said anything, and Maggie had a feeling it was because no one wanted to agree with her, especially since what she said was true.

"And he hates me for keeping him away from Summer!" Blair cried, obviously feeling the lack of support in the room.

"But I didn't shoot anyone. I wouldn't," Tyler protested. "I don't even own a gun."

Sam stepped forward and took Tyler's elbow. "Let's go have a chat, Tyler."

"Maggie, do something," Tyler pleaded as Sam started to lead him away. "I only came here to help you."

"He did," Maggie said. But suddenly, nothing was as it seemed, and her voice lost its conviction as she added, "We came by to pick up the desks."

Sam gave her a sympathetic glance, as if he knew she was reeling.

"That'll have to wait for another time. Deputy Wilson, take a statement from Blair, would you?" Sam asked. "I'm going to take Tyler in back."

"You're not arresting him, are you?" Maggie asked.

"Yes, of course he is," Blair said. "He tried to kill me. He's your suspect. He probably killed Bruce, too, to exact his revenge upon me. Oh, my poor, darling Bruce."

Blair began to sob and wail. Summer put a reluctant arm around her mother's shoulder and offered her comfort. Her eyes stayed on Tyler, however, and she looked stricken.

"I didn't kill Bruce!" Tyler argued. "I swear! Summer, you have to believe me!"

"I do," Summer said. "I do believe you."

Blair let out an outraged gasp and, at that point, everyone started yelling. Maggie saw Blair's driver break free of her hold and bolt for the door. She thought he had the right idea but knew she'd never get away with it.

An ear-piercing whistle was emitted over the shrieks and yells, and it had everyone clapping their hands over their ears. Dot lowered the two fingers from her mouth and pointed for Sam and Tyler to go to the back. Neither of them said a word. They just went.

Once they were out of sight, Dot spoke, "If you ladies would come with me, I'll take down your statement, Blair."

"What can I do?" Maggie asked.

"Oh, I think you've done enough," Summer snapped. "Your man is about to arrest mine for a murder he didn't commit. Are you satisfied now?"

Maggie threw her hands up in the air. Wasn't that nice? Here she was trying to help the ungrateful woman and all she got for it was attitude.

And while, yes, she had to admit the whole thing had blown up on her, she really felt that her intentions should count for something, shouldn't they?

Apparently not, since Dot took Summer and her mother to another room in the back, leaving Maggie standing alone in the front of the station. Pulling her gloves and hat out of her pockets, she yanked them on before she headed out into the cold to walk back to her shop.

"Do you think Tyler did it?" Ginger asked over a steaming cup of hot chocolate.

Maggie had brewed a large pot of the bad mood elixir in the break room, which was in reality just a counter in the storeroom, in anticipation of her friends' arrival. It was the best recipe in the world, which Sam had gotten from his cousin, a restaurant owner in Massachusetts—with cinnamon sticks, nutmeg and vanilla, there was no foul mood that this recipe couldn't cure.

Well, except for maybe Tyler Fawkes's current bad

mood. Maggie had debated bringing him some cocoa, but since Dot had texted her that Sam was keeping him in the jail as a person of interest, she didn't think cocoa was going to help Tyler. Not right now, at any rate.

"No, I don't think Tyler did it," Maggie said. "Well, maybe? No, no, definitely not!"

"Well, that was conclusive," Ginger said.

They were sitting in the comfy seats in the lounge area of Maggie's shop. She had closed for the evening, but they were waiting for Claire to join them so that they could go over their Presidents' Day shopping plan. Maggie and Ginger had already scoured the flyers and determined which stores to hit in what order, but they wanted Claire's input as well.

"I just can't imagine that he would. I mean, Tyler's the original gentle giant. He looks scary, but he's really a big teddy bear," Maggie said. "Then again, Blair did break them up."

"But to whack Bruce with a hammer?" Ginger asked. "I just don't see it."

"I know," Maggie said. "I've been afraid to call Sam, as I really am trying to mind my own business."

Ginger raised her eyebrows. A knock on the glass door sounded before she could say anything, for which Maggie was relieved. She felt bad enough about today's debacle without adding Ginger's worries for her and Sam on top of it.

She hurried to the door and unlocked it, pushing it open so Claire could come in. She brought with her a nip of cold, and Ginger was already pouring a hot chocolate for her as she took a seat and began to unwrap herself from her hat, scarf, gloves and coat.

"What a day, huh?" Claire asked.

"And then some," Maggie said.

Claire cupped her mug of chocolate and blew on it. "I have news."

"Yes?" Ginger and Maggie asked together.

"Tyler has an alibi for Bruce's murder," she said. "Pete told me over dinner."

Now why didn't Sam tell me that? Maggie asked.

"Hush," Ginger shushed her. "What alibi?"

"This is the best part," Claire said. Then she took a long sip of her cocoa.

"Oh, come on," Maggie said. "You're killing me here."

Both Ginger and Claire looked at her.

"Sorry, bad choice of words," she said.

"Well, Tyler couldn't have murdered Bruce, because he was using his truck to help Doc Franklin move back home," Claire said.

"Doc and Alice are back together?" Ginger asked. "No kidding?"

"Word on the street is that Doc pulled out all the stops on Valentine's Day and wore Alice down," Claire said. "Apparently, the gazebo was all decorated, and he saw it and used it as a place to plead his case."

Maggie smiled. Sam would be happy to hear that the gazebo had helped Doc out, too.

She took a long sip of her hot chocolate and then heaved a sigh of relief. Doc Franklin had been Maggie's boss for over twenty years, as she had done the medical billing for his small practice since she was in high school.

Doc and Alice had been like a second family to Maggie and her daughter, and when they had split up a few months ago, Maggie had taken it harder than anyone save the two of them.

She felt a lump in her throat and had to swallow before she could speak. "That's great news. Really great."

"Well, for Tyler's sake, the timing couldn't have been better," Claire said. "Doc gave a sworn statement that Tyler was with him all day hauling furniture."

"Thank goodness," Ginger said. "Of course, that doesn't mean he didn't shoot at Blair."

"No, and two witnesses have said they saw his truck speed through town at the time of the shooting," Claire said.

"Is Sam still holding him?" Maggie asked.

"He has to," Claire said. "More for Tyler's sake than anything else. Sam told Pete when he came to get his afternoon coffee that if another move is made on Blair, that'll set Tyler free. He's also assigned Dot to be Blair's shadow until Bruce's murderer is caught. So it sounds like Sam doesn't think it's Tyler but is trying to help him out."

"I wonder if Tyler sees it that way," Ginger said.

"I don't know, but I'm trying to picture Dot and Blair together twenty-four/seven. That's going to be interesting," Maggie said.

"I wonder if Dot is getting hazard pay," Ginger said.

"What did you discover from looking over the Cassidy finances?" Maggie asked Ginger.

"Not much more than the fact that they are loaded," Ginger said. "I'd need more access to their accounts to dig deeper, but from what I could tell, Bruce and Blair Cassidy lived large and liked it that way."

"Was there any indication of who would profit from Bruce's death?" Maggie asked. Ginger and Claire both looked at her. "Other than Blair and Summer?"

"If Sela Cassidy is Bruce's first wife and she can be found, she would be it. But there's no financial record of her anywhere. It's as if she vanished, so I don't know," Ginger said.

"With a court order, Sam can do a much more detailed search, but as far as I could see in the public records databases I accessed, Bruce had no other heirs," Claire said.

"What do we know about Sela?" Maggie asked. "Did she have any family?"

"Maggie Gerber!" a voice barked from the door. "What part of 'butt out' are you not getting?"

Maggie jumped at the male voice, then she put her hand over her chest to calm her rioting heart.

"You sounded just like Sam and you almost gave me a heart attack," she said. "That was not funny, Maxwell Button!"

"Well, neither is leaving your door unlocked when there is a murderer on the loose," Max said. "I have a good mind to tell Sam how irresponsible you're being."

"Blah, blah, blah." Maggie waved him off. "Hollow threats will not get you hot chocolate."

"Homemade with marshmallows?" he asked.

"Mmm-hmm," Maggie murmured.

"Fine, I'll quit badgering." Max stomped across the floor toward the sitting area.

"And you won't tell Sam," Maggie said.

"Fine," he agreed. "Now pony up the goods."

Tall and lanky, Max appeared to be all arms and legs, but he wore a well-cut navy suit that gave him a few more manly angles, and his black hair, which used to hang over his face, was neatly trimmed and professional-looking. Maggie couldn't help but marvel at how her young friend had cleaned up once he found the motivation in the form of a lovely young woman named Bianca Madison.

Maxwell Button was St. Stanley's resident genius. A throwaway kid with super smarts, the entire town, particularly Claire, had helped raise him, and now at the age of twenty, he had a law degree and had passed the bar as well as an advanced degree for any other subject that had caught his fancy, of which there were many.

"How's school going?" Claire asked him.

Claire and Max had a long history, since Claire was the one who had found him squatting in the town library when he was a teen and had been pivotal in getting him back in school. When she discovered his smarts were off the chart, she helped him to get a job and find a place to live as well.

Sadly, Max's own parents were not involved in their son's life, preferring their isolated existence in their trailer on the outskirts of town. It had been Claire who guided Max's journey to college, especially the pursuit of his law degree.

"I'm almost finished," he said. "I just have to write my dissertation."

Ginger poured him a mug of cocoa and pushed the bag of marshmallows at him.

"Remind me again why an attorney needs an art history degree?" she asked.

He grinned. "It helps keep my brain sharp."

"Any other advanced degrees in the offing, boy genius?" Maggie asked.

"That's man genius now," he corrected her. "No, in fact, I'm looking to take on a new position altogether."

"But I thought you liked working for Judge Harding," Maggie said.

"I do. It's not that position that I'm looking to change," he said. "I'm sort of hoping for a promotion elsewhere, if you get my drift."

Maggie glanced at Ginger and Claire. They were as perplexed as she was. The three of them looked at him with matching puzzled expressions; clearly, they had no idea what he was talking about. Goodness, she hoped he wasn't going back to delivering pizza and working at the Frosty Freeze again.

"Here, I'll show you," he said. Max reached into his jacket pocket and pulled out a small burgundy velvet box.

Chapter 20

Maggie, Claire and Ginger gasped as one. Max looked up with wide eyes. "What? Is there a spider on me?"

"Max!" They wailed in unison.

He grinned, then he looked nervous. "Okay, you have to tell me if you think Bianca will like it."

He popped the lid and Maggie felt her jaw drop. The others were silent as they took in the sight of the sparkly before them.

"Well, what do you think?" he asked. His voice was tense, as if he was fearing the worst.

"Oh, my eyes, my eyes," Maggie cried as she threw up her hands to shield her view.

"All I can see are spots!" Ginger said. "It's like staring at the sun."

Claire laughed and reached forward to take the box from Max's hand and look at the ring more closely.

"Max, it's stunning," she said.

Max met Claire's gaze, and for just a nanosecond he looked wistful. Max had carried a torch for the librarian since she'd stepped into his life as a teen, but then he had met and fallen for Bianca, leaving his crush on the older woman behind. Maggie and Ginger exchanged a glance and she knew Ginger had noted the same thing she had.

"It's perfect for Bianca," Claire said. "She's going to love it."

"Thanks," Max said. He grinned, and the moment between them passed like a whisper on the wind.

Maggie took the small box from Claire to see the dazzler more clearly. A large, round diamond was nestled in a ring of channel-set sapphires in a platinum band. It truly was magnificent.

She handed it to Ginger so she could see it, too.

"How did you manage to pay for that?" Maggie asked. "Sell a kidney?"

"Close," he said. "I financed most of it, but I got the down payment by agreeing to become Blair Cassidy's personal attorney."

"Oh, wow, are you sure you wouldn't rather give up a kidney?" Ginger asked. "If Bianca ever doubts your love for her, you can just trot out that little detail and all her fears will be laid to rest."

"I had hoped you'd be willing to represent Summer if she needed it. Is that what Blair hired you for?" Maggie asked.

"No, she's convinced Tyler killed Bruce despite his having an alibi, so she doesn't think she'll need me to represent Summer," Max said and shook his head, letting them know what he thought about that. "What Mrs. Cassidy wants me to look at is her estate from Bruce Cassidy. Apparently, he kept all of the financials to himself, so she has no idea how much money she has or where it is or anything."

"Ugh!" Claire shuddered. "That's positively barbaric. I could never not know my finances down to the penny."

Maggie and Ginger nodded. Maybe it was because she was a Good Buy Girl, or perhaps because she'd been on her own for so long, but either way, the thought of not being in control of her own money made Maggie queasy.

"Which is another reason I stopped by," Max said. He turned to Ginger. "Since financial statements are not my area of expertise, I was wondering if you'd be willing to offer some insight?"

"Absolutely," Ginger said without hesitation. "I'd be happy to help."

Maggie opened her mouth to mention that Ginger had already started, but Ginger shot her a look that said "hush." Maggie did.

"So, when are you going to ask Bianca to marry you?" Ginger asked.

"I thought I'd pop the question when I got home tonight," he said.

"Tonight?" Claire sputtered.

"Just like that?" Maggie asked.

"With no candlelight dinner or flowers or anything?" Ginger asked.

"I kind of thought the ring was enough," Max said. He looked put out. "You know, along with pledging my life to hers, like, forever."

"For a man with all that fancy-shmancy education, you're dumb as a brick in the romance department," Maggie said.

Max gasped as if she'd slapped him. "Ouch!"

"Where's the creativity? Where's the thoughtfulness? Where's the romance?" Maggie cried.

"Really?" a voice asked from the door. "I just got here. Can't I even take off my jacket before I trot out the romance? And why is the door unlocked when we have a murderer running around?"

They all glanced over to see Sam shutting the door behind him.

"Sam, you're just in time," Claire said.

"Yes," Ginger agreed. "We need a man to help us head off this disaster."

Sam looked immediately alert. "Is there a crime happening?"

"No, but there will be if you don't back us up," Maggie said.

Sam looked perplexed as he sat down on the love seat beside her. He draped his arm around her shoulders and planted a kiss on her hair before he turned to Max.

"What did you do?" he asked him.

"What?" Max raised his hands in a gesture of innocence. "What makes you think it's me?"

"You're the only dude in the room; it has to be something you did," Sam said.

Max heaved a sigh. He held out the box for Sam to see, and Sam gave a low whistle.

"You got that legit, right?" he asked. "I'm not going to have to haul you in for burglary, am I?"

"Yes!" Max said. "If you consider selling your soul to the devil legit. I even have the receipt. That's not the problem."

Sam frowned. "She didn't say no, did she? A fine guy like you, she'd be crazy to turn you down."

Max grinned, and Maggie leaned into Sam. She liked the way he made Max feel good about himself. Max hadn't had a lot of that in his life.

"No. They're saying my planned proposal lacks romance, creativity and thoughtfulness," he said.

"Oh." Sam puckered his lips. "What was your plan?"

"I was just going to lob it out there," Max said. "And see how she answered."

"Lob it out there?" Ginger asked.

"This isn't softball," Claire said.

"I have to give them that," Sam said. "This is the big leagues. You need to make it memorable."

"Aw, what?" Max asked. "But I'm no good at that mushy emotional stuff."

"We'll help you," Maggie said. She reached over and patted his knee. "Maybe you should start by calling Laura. She and Bianca are friends; maybe she'd have some ideas for you."

"Well, where am I going to keep the ring in the mean-time?" Max asked. "If she finds it, it's game over."

"You can keep it in my safe," Maggie said. "It's bolted

to the floor in back, and I'm the only one who knows the combination."

"Okay," Max said with a heavy sigh. He slapped the box into Maggie's palm. He rose to his feet and they all joined him. "I was really looking forward to seeing her face, though. Are you sure I can't—?"

"Yes, we're sure," Claire said. She turned to Ginger and Maggie. "Can you e-mail me our itinerary for shopping the sales? I need to get my game face on, and knowing our agenda will help. Shoot, maybe by then we'll know if we're shopping for pink or blue."

"I'll send it as soon as I get home," Ginger said.

While Maggie went to lock up the ring, Sam let the others out. She was just closing the safe when Sam arrived in the break room with the tray of mugs and the pot of chocolate.

He began rinsing and washing at the small sink, and Maggie stepped up to help him. "I do love this domestic side to you, Sheriff Collins."

"Maybe Max should propose while doing dishes," he said.

Maggie laughed. She felt Sam watching her and turned to find him staring at her with an intensity that made her dizzy.

"Would that work?" he asked.

"I . . . uh," she stuttered, and then she caught on that he was teasing her. She flicked her dish towel at him. "Quit messing with me."

He turned away and began to hum while he scrubbed the last of the mugs, leaving Maggie utterly boggled.

What had that been about? Did Sam want to get married? Oh no, did that mean he wanted kids, too? She supposed they should have *the talk*. If he wanted kids, then she really had to cut him loose. It just wasn't fair to keep him from having his own family just because she'd already done the domestic diva routine.

She could picture him with a pretty young wife and their two kids, holding hands while they walked down Main Street as a cute family unit. The idea depressed her more than she thought was possible.

"Hey, you look like you just lost your best friend," Sam said. "What's the matter?"

She glanced up at him. His words were closer to the mark than he knew. Over the past few months, he really had become her best friend.

She shook her head. "Nothing. I'm just fretting."

"So you need something else to think about," he said. He wiggled his eyebrows at her. "I think I have just the thing in mind."

With a laugh, she let him pull her into his arms. If she was going to have to let him go, then she was determined to enjoy every second she had with him now.

Maggie hurried into the Daily Grind for her afternoon cup of go juice. She'd been fighting a case of the yawns and she knew the only thing that would fix it was a brisk walk in the February air followed by an extra large cup of Pete's coffee.

When she stepped into the shop, however, she found

Max and Ginger ensconced at a wall table with their laptops open and the table littered with muffin wrappers and ceramic mugs of coffee.

"Hi, guys," she said as she approached. "Whatcha doin'?"

Ginger glanced up at her. Her eyes looked partially glazed and Maggie was sure it took her a second or two to place her.

"Ginger, it's me, your BFF, Maggie," she said.

Ginger rubbed her eyes with her fingers. "Sorry, I knew it was you. I just crawled out of a labyrinth of financials that are making my head ache."

"Tell me about it," Max muttered. "I think it's time to call Sam."

"Why?" Maggie asked. "Did you find something?"

Max and Ginger exchanged a look. It was a guarded look, as if they weren't sure of how much to say. Maggie tried not to be offended, but she couldn't help but feel a bit excluded.

"Tell him we're going to need to talk to Blair," Ginger said. "She must understand some of this."

That was it. Maggie sat down. She was not moving until they told her what they'd uncovered. She'd go into full-on student protest limp body mode if she must.

Max nodded and tapped his phone. He raised it up to his ear. "It's Max . . . Yeah, we found some interesting stuff . . . How do you feel about monthly deposits to an account in Switzerland?"

Max was silent for a long moment. "We're at the Daily Grind. Yeah, she'd better come, too."

Max put his phone down. "Sam is on his way, and he's bringing Blair."

Ginger looked pained but resigned.

"So you are officially working the case now?" Maggie asked her friend, trying to keep the jealous note out of her voice.

"Yes, Max asked Blair to give me broader access to their financials," Ginger said. "It was a dogfight, but she finally agreed."

"And thank goodness for that," Max said. "You get this stuff so much better than I do."

"And that's saying something," Maggie said. Ginger flushed with pleasure.

"I'm just happy to help," she said. She glanced out the window that overlooked the town green. "I'll do anything to help catch a killer on the loose."

Seeing Maggie, Pete came out from behind the counter and approached the table. He was wearing his usual green apron with the shop's logo on the bib, and his happy-go-lucky smile was firmly in place.

"I've got one for you," he said. "What did one cup of coffee say to another?"

Maggie braced herself. Pete loved to tell coffee-oriented jokes, but you never knew how it was going to go. The only person who laughed every single time was Claire.

"No idea," she said.

"Where you bean?" he asked. He busted out a belly laugh, which was contagious and made Maggie laugh harder than the joke had.

Ginger shook her head at him. "That was not any funnier the second time around."

"Maggie laughed," Pete protested. "And you should have heard Claire. She laughed and laughed."

"That's because she's in love with you," Max said. Maggie was pleased that he sounded so okay with it.

"Yeah," Pete agreed, and the smile he gave them was blinding. "So, the usual high octane, Maggie?"

"Yes, please," she said as she stifled a yawn. She had asked Mrs. Kellerman from the dry cleaner's next door to watch her shop, and she really needed to get back, but she also wanted to see Sam, even if it was just for a moment.

Pete returned to his counter, and Maggie wondered if she should have asked for even higher octane, but she didn't want to get the shakes.

"Late night last night?" Ginger asked her. Her voice was laced with innuendo, and Maggie felt her face grow warm.

"I had insomnia," she said.

"Really?" Ginger asked. "I thought his name was Sam."

"Good one!" Max snorted and held up a hand to high-five Ginger. When they were done laughing, Maggie gave him a frosty look.

"Just remember I am the keeper of all that sparkles," she said. "You would do well to stay on my good side so I don't shut you down."

"Noted," Max said, abruptly serious.

Pete returned with a large cup of coffee for Maggie just as the door opened and Sam entered the shop with Blair and Summer. Maggie hadn't seen either of them since the unfortunate encounter in the front of the police station. She wondered if maybe she should have left while the leaving was good.

Sure enough, Blair glanced from Sam to Maggie and snapped, "What is *she* doing here?"

Sam glanced at Maggie, who held up her cup as her first line of defense. He smiled.

"I don't know," he said. "But, as always, I am delighted to see her."

Chapter 21

"I refuse to discuss my case with her here," Blair said.

She looked as if she were going to dig her spiky heels into Pete's wood floor. Maggie rose from her seat. She wasn't going to cause a scene just because she might die of curiosity.

"Mama, stop it!" Summer snapped. "Maggie and her people have been really helpful to us, and you're being just awful."

"Ah!" Blair gasped. "How could you? How could you side with them against your own mama?"

"Because without them, I would be up for murder," Summer said. "That's how I could. Now, please, sit down and shut up."

Maggie glanced at Summer in surprise. She had gone

from accusing Maggie of shooting her mother to getting Tyler arrested for defending her. Frankly, it was getting hard to keep up with the woman's moods. She wondered if this was part of her appeal to Tyler. His personality was pretty much steady as it goes. Maybe Summer goosed that a bit for him.

The fire in Summer's eyes must have clued Blair in to the seriousness of her words, because Blair let out an indignant huff and stomped forward clutching her arm in its sling close to her chest.

Max hastily stood up and pulled out a chair for her. Blair sank into it as if she was about to expire at any moment.

Sam pulled up a chair from another table and wedged it in next to Maggie's while Summer took the remaining seat.

"I can go," Maggie said. "I was only passing by and saw Max and Ginger. I need to get back anyway. I don't want to abuse Mrs. Kellerman's generosity in watching the shop."

Sam looked at her and shook his head. "No, you're good. After careful consideration, I think it's safer to have you in the loop than out."

"Because I'm so insightful and helpful?" she asked.

"More accurately, so you don't go rogue on me and get yourself killed," he said.

Maggie gave him a small smile. She knew that he really didn't want her involved but that he was beginning to understand that in a community this small, everyone was involved. He squeezed her knee and then turned to the table.

"All right, Ginger, tell us what you know," he said.

Ginger frowned. "First, I have to ask Blair and Summer a few questions. To start with, did Bruce go to Switzerland often?"

Blair raised her eyebrows in surprise. "No, he hated traveling. He was deathly afraid of flying. We had to drive everywhere. He didn't even own a passport."

"Huh," Ginger said as she looked back down at her papers. "Did he have family over there?"

"No, he had no family."

"Did he own a business?"

"In Switzerland?" Blair asked. She sounded exasperated. "No! Why?"

"Are you absolutely sure?" Ginger asked.

"Yes, I'm positive. I was married to him, after all," Blair said. "I would think I would know if he was doing business in a foreign country, wouldn't I?"

Ginger closed her eyes and took a deep breath through her nose as if she was gathering every ounce of patience she possessed. She slowly exhaled through her mouth and opened her eyes.

"Okay, this is going to be more difficult than I thought," Ginger said. She gave Max an apologetic look and he nodded.

"Why do you keep asking about Switzerland?" Blair asked.

"Oh, you mean you *don't* know?" Ginger asked.

"Know what?" Blair growled. "What are you not telling me?"

"Well, as you said, you were married to him, so one

would think you'd know that he was sending money to Switzerland every month." Ginger paused to give her a pointed look. "Oh, and maybe you could tell us why. You were married to him, after all."

"Money?" Blair asked. Ginger's sarcasm was lost on her. The details of her money being sent out of the country, however, were not. "My money was being sent to Switzerland every month?"

"Yes, Bruce sent several thousand dollars to Switzerland every month for the past ten years," Ginger said. "Although it gets a bit spotty about two years ago—Bruce started sending less, and not as regularly."

"That would be when we got married," Blair said. She studied the large diamond on her ring finger. "Bruce liked to buy me pretty things, and he did once say something about having to reallocate his funds if he was going to keep me happy."

Maggie glanced at Summer, who was looking at her mother with a tiny frown marring her forehead. She got the feeling that Summer was seeing her mother and her mother's life choices clearly for the very first time.

"Don't frown, dear," Blair chastised her daughter. "You'll wrinkle."

Summer let out a sigh worthy of a teen in the rocky throes of adolescence. Maggie felt sorry for her. Henpecked and nitpicked her entire life by Blair—was it any wonder Summer had turned out as she had?

"Is there any way to tell who or what the money was going to?" Sam asked.

"No, the Swiss bank privacy laws are pretty strict about that sort of thing," Ginger said. "They won't even verify the account. I only know of its existence because Bruce left a paper trail on this end."

"Blair, I know you refuse to accept that Bruce was married before you," Sam said. "But you have to consider that the money he was sending to this Swiss account was for Sela Cassidy, his first wife. It makes sense that she'd be in Europe, as she was a professional downhill skier until she blew out one of her knees. It could be that they are legitimately divorced and this is alimony. We just haven't found the paperwork yet."

Blair's eyebrows lowered, and her mouth turned up on one side in a snarl.

"He was never married before," she said. "Why won't anyone believe me?"

"Because it doesn't make any sense, Mama," Summer said. Her tone was gentle. "I know you want to believe that you were his only wife, but you have to see that there were things Bruce didn't tell you, and it looks like having a previous wife and depositing money in a foreign bank account were two of them."

Blair blinked and turned to her daughter with large, sad eyes. "But he told me that I was the only woman he had ever married. Why would he lie?"

Summer shrugged. "I don't know. Men lie. It's what they do."

Sam and Max cleared their throats and Ginger said, "Present company excepted, of course."

They looked somewhat mollified. Maggie could feel Sam's gaze on her, and she squeezed his hand to assure him that she did not think like that.

"I just don't understand," Blair sobbed as she leaned heavily on Summer's shoulder. "He could have told me he was married before. I wouldn't judge. I mean, it's not like I was a virgin bride."

Maggie choked on her coffee and Blair shot her a nasty look.

"Sorry, wrong pipe," she said. Ginger glanced away and Maggie knew she was trying not to laugh.

Sam's phone buzzed and he took it out of his pocket. Glancing at the display, he stood and said, "Excuse me. I have to take this."

He stepped away from the table, and Maggie watched him go. His body was outlined by the window, and she admired his straight posture and broad shoulders. Although the years were beginning to tell, with the start of wrinkles and gray hair, he was just as handsome as he'd been when they were in high school.

"Isn't that right, Maggie?" Max asked.

Hearing her name, Maggie turned back to the table with an undignified, "Huh? What?"

"I was saying that it's in Blair's best interest for Cassidy to have been married before," Max said.

"How do you figure that?" Blair asked. She looked cranky.

"Because it gives us someone to look for who may have wanted to murder him."

Blair blanched, and Max looked contrite.

"Sorry, that was tactless of me," he said. "But you see my point."

"No, it's not that," Blair said. "Well, it was tactless, but that's not why I'm upset."

"What is it, Mama?" Summer asked.

"If he lied to me about being married, how do I know he didn't lie to me about other things?" she asked. "What if he has children out there? Or siblings? Or parents? Heavens, there could be a whole entourage of Cassidys that I'm going to have to deal with."

"Anything is possible," Summer said. "But hiding an ex-wife is one thing; hiding children would be much more difficult."

"Agreed," Ginger said. "And as a mother of four, I know what I'm talking about."

"I hope you're right," Blair said. "Because I am not sharing my inheritance with any surprise snot-nosed brats."

More than anything else, her incredible selfishness reassured Maggie that Blair was fine. If there was one truth about Blair, it was that she would always look out for her own interests first and everyone else's second.

"Mama, that's not very nice," Summer chastised her mother.

"I'm not trying to be nice. And if anyone tries to take what's mine they're going to see just how not nice I can be," Blair said.

Summer sighed, and Max frowned and said, "That's the sort of comment you might want to hold in so as not to look too greedy when we go to probate."

Now it was Blair's turn to look put-upon. Maggie didn't think she was up for any more histrionics. She glanced back at Sam and saw him slip his phone back into his pocket. He looked grim when he approached the table.

"Well, Blair, it appears you were right," Sam said. "Your husband wasn't married before you."

Blair tossed her black bob and looked vindicated. "I knew it. I was Bruce's one true love. He always said so."

"Well, that's where it gets a bit more interesting," Sam said.

They all turned to look at him as he resumed his seat at the table.

"You weren't married to Bruce Cassidy," he said. "You were married to a man named Terry Knox."

Chapter 22

"That's impossible," Blair said. She looked at Sam as if he were a complete idiot. "Honestly, do you even know what you are doing? A first wife, foreign bank accounts, and now you say his name isn't his. It's like you're not investigating my husband's murder at all."

"Blair, as far as I know, I am now investigating the murder of a man named Terry Knox. Whether he was really your husband or not, I don't know," Sam said. "The medical examiner matched the fingerprints of our victim to those of a man named Terry Knox whose last known residence was in San Diego, California. That's the same city your husband was from, yes?"

Blair looked horrified. She turned to Summer, who

looked equally stunned. Then she turned back to Sam and said, "Yes, Bruce was from San Diego. He said he was retired military and had a small cottage just north of the city on the water."

"Well, his fingerprints identify him as someone else entirely. I'm going back to the station to see what I can find out about Terry Knox," Sam said. His voice was gentle when he continued, "Blair, I suggest you find any documentation you can about your husband. Birth certificate, marriage license, driver's license—anything that might help us unravel this mess."

"We have a safe-deposit box at the bank," she said. "Bruce rented it when we arrived in town."

"I'm going to need to see the contents," Sam said. "I'll have Deputy Wilson go with you to the bank."

"I'll come, too," Summer said.

"Contact me at the station if you need anything," Sam said. He rose from his seat, and Maggie rose with him.

"I'll walk with you," she said. "I need to get back to the shop."

"I'm going to call Judge Harding," Max said. "He might be able to give us some direction as to what to do next, because if you weren't even married to Bruce Cassidy, then you're not really his widow—"

Blair let loose with a wail that could have shattered glass. With an apologetic wave to Pete behind the counter and to the others, Sam and Maggie beat feet toward the door. Once outside, they didn't slow down, but hurried away as if fleeing the scene of a crime.

"Scale of one to ten," Maggie huffed as they hurried

down the street, "how mad do you think Ginger will be at me for leaving her in that train wreck?"

"Max convinced Blair to hire Ginger to go through the financials, right?" Sam asked as he grabbed her hand and guided her across the street.

"Right," Maggie said as she stepped up onto the curb beside him.

"Then she's getting paid, so she really can't complain, now can she?"

"I suppose not."

"Text me when you get to the shop," he said.

Maggie looked at him in question.

"I worry," he said. "There's a murderer out there, and now our vic isn't who he seems, making it even more curious, not to mention dangerous."

"You love this stuff, don't you?" she asked. There was no way he could deny the sparkle in his eye as he tried to figure out what exactly was happening in their sleepy little town.

"I'm not happy that someone was murdered, but I'm damn determined to catch the killer," he said.

"I'll text you," Maggie said. "Promise."

"Thanks."

He paused to plant a quick kiss on her lips before turning down the sidewalk that would take him to the station while she continued on to her shop. A few steps away and Maggie turned back and grabbed his hand, stopping him.

"I worry, too, just so you know," she said, squeezing his fingers with hers. "Please be careful."

"I promise," he said. "I have an awful lot to live for

and I don't intend to let anything mess it up. I'll swing by the shop later." Then he stopped and leveled her with an intense stare. "I love you, Maggie."

"I love you, too," she said.

She gave him a quick wave and then hurried toward her shop. Maybe it was the weird twist the case had taken, but Maggie couldn't help but feel creeped out that there was a murderer among them who had successfully bludgeoned one person and nearly shot another to death.

Was Blair their target, and if so, why? And if Terry Knox really wasn't Bruce Cassidy, then why was he murdered? Was it someone out to get Bruce Cassidy or Terry Knox? Maggie's head was spinning with questions, but with no more information, she couldn't even hazard a guess. It was maddening.

Maggie spent the afternoon wondering what, if anything, Sam had discovered about Terry Knox. She hadn't heard from Ginger, and she worried about that, too. Blair was high maintenance on a normal day; Maggie could only imagine what she was like now.

Thankfully, Ginger arrived just before Maggie was about to close the shop, with Claire in tow. One look at her face and Maggie knew the day had been a long one. Ginger collapsed onto the couch and flung her forearm over her forehead. She was the picture of distress.

"Rough day?" Maggie asked.

"Nothing a tranquilizer gun couldn't have cured," Ginger said. "Pity I don't carry one."

Claire pushed her black-framed glasses up onto her nose and nodded in agreement.

"Apparently, Blair is not processing the news that her husband wasn't who she thought he was very well," she said. "Max stopped by the library to do some research after he dropped Blair and Summer off at Doc Franklin's. He was hoping Doc could help ease Blair's panic attack."

"Since my phone stopped ringing incessantly about an hour ago, I'd say he succeeded," Ginger said. "Remind me to bake Doc Franklin a pound cake."

"Why was your phone ringing?" Claire asked.

"Well, after the sheriff and company ditched us in the coffee shop," Ginger said with a pointed look at Maggie, who gave a sheepish shrug, "Blair went right into full-on money panic mode."

"She's afraid she's going to lose it all?" Maggie guessed.

"You got it," Ginger said. "If Terry Knox stole Bruce Cassidy's identity as well as all of his money, then there really isn't anything for her to inherit, especially if their marriage was a fraud."

"Wow, if her marriage is invalid, she loses it all?" Claire said. "That is a huge kick in the pants."

"Especially, if you're as used to spending money as she is," Ginger said. "Honestly, going over her financials has been eye-opening to say the least."

"I take it Blair is not up for membership in the Good Buy Girls?" Maggie asked.

"Huh," Ginger huffed. "She may have to have an initiation by fire."

Claire wrinkled her nose. "Thrift is a gift—either you have it or you don't."

"It's true," Ginger said. "You can imitate but never replicate the skills of those blessed in the consumer arts."

Maggie laughed, not only at Ginger's words but at the thought of Blair Cassidy buying anything on sale ever. It boggled.

Claire's phone chimed, and so did Ginger's. Maggie knew immediately what that meant. She raced to the break room to grab her purse, and sure enough, there was a text from Michael. He and Joanne were on their way to the hospital—again.

Maggie hurried back into the shop. She glanced at the others to see that they were already headed toward the door.

"Maybe we should order a pizza," Claire said. "Probably this is false labor again, and a pizza will cheer Joanne up more than hugs at the end of this ordeal."

"Agreed," Ginger said. "Last week she was craving anchovies—bleck. Is she over that?"

"Yes, I think she's moved on to green olives and sausage," Maggie said as she locked the door behind them.

"My car?" Ginger asked.

Maggie and Claire followed her to her minivan. They hurriedly got in, and Maggie took her phone out to text Sam. Since they were supposed to meet up later, she wanted him to know what was happening so that he didn't worry.

Claire took her phone out, too, and ordered a pizza to be delivered to the maternity ward.

"Done," she said. "And I asked for extra olives."

They zipped into the visitor's lot at the hospital and together they hurried up to the third floor. The woman at the information desk was used to seeing them by now, and she waved at them as they passed.

"Tell Joanne and Michael we're all rooting for them," she said.

Maggie and the others waved in acknowledgment. Once in the large waiting room, Ginger went to verify that Joanne was already there, and the maternity ward nurse confirmed that she had just been brought in.

They were the only ones in the waiting room, so they took over the television, turning on a romantic comedy while thumbing through the magazines. The pizza arrived, and they had just tucked into it when the doors to the ward burst open and Michael appeared.

"Oh, no, not again," Claire said. "Poor Joanne, is she terribly disappointed?"

"No, in fact, I just came out to tell you that she's dilated to five centimeters and one hundred percent effaced. We're having this baby!" Michael cried.

The three of them erupted from their seats and began to jump up and down.

"Dilated and effaced is good, right?" Claire asked, still jumping with the others. Ginger burst out laughing and wrapped her arms around Claire.

"It's wonderful," she said. "That baby has finally made up its mind to join us."

"Can we see her?" Maggie asked. She wiped her pizza fingers on a napkin, trying to clean up to go into the ward.

"You know what they say," Ginger said. "It's easier to seek forgiveness than permission. Let's just go. They'll kick us out if they have to."

Michael led the way back through the doors to the ward. Given the late hour, it was quiet. The occasional cry of a baby was the only loud noise, and it mingled with the muted sound of the televisions in the birthing rooms.

At the end of the corridor, he turned right and pushed through a wide swinging door.

Half sitting, hugging her big belly with her arms, was Joanne.

"Hee hee hee hi," she said. "The baby's . . . hee hee . . . coming."

"Oh my god!" Claire cried. "This is so exciting! Can I get you anything? What do you need? Are you in pain?"

Ginger and Maggie exchanged a glance. Joanne's dark brown hair was up on her head in its usual ponytail, but strands heavy with sweat had escaped the elastic and were plastered to her neck and the sides of her face. As to Claire's last question, Maggie had no doubt Joanne was in excruciating pain.

"No, nothing, a little bit," Joanne answered in between breaths.

Ginger moved in close and gave her a solid hug. Claire was next, and then Maggie.

"You're doing great," Maggie said. "Just keep breathing."

"Did you have an epidural with Laura?" Joanne asked.

"Yes," she said.

"What about you . . . hee hee . . . Ginger?" Joanne asked.

"For the first two," she said. "The second two just sort of fell out when I sneezed."

Claire looked horrified, but Maggie laughed. "I remember that. Forty-five minutes of labor and *bang*— baby."

"It was crazy," Ginger said. "We were sure Dante was going to be born in the car. As it was, we just made it through the front door when he started to crown."

"I wanted . . . hee hee . . . to have a natural childbirth," Joanne said. "But there's one thing they don't tell you."

"What's that?" Claire asked.

"It hurts like—"

The machine that Joanne was hooked up to let out a chirping noise, cutting off what she was about to say. Maggie watched the monitor.

"What's happening?" Claire asked. Her eyes were huge as Michael elbowed his way back to his wife's side and took her hand in his.

"She's having a contraction," Ginger said. "It'll pass."

"Unnngh!" Joanne let out a growling grunt that sounded as if it came all the way up from her toes.

"We'd better leave them to it," Maggie said. She stepped up to Joanne's other side and quickly kissed her head. "We're here if you need us."

Ginger moved in after her and did the same. "Keep breathing, honey. Your sweet bundle is on its way."

Joanne gave her a smile that was more bared teeth than upturned lips, but Ginger had been through it four times herself and knew the drill.

"Go, girl!" Claire said. She glanced at Joanne's belly, which, even under her hospital johnnie, looked rock hard in the midst of her contraction. Claire stepped back as if the condition were contagious. She slapped Michael on the back and said, "Take care of our girl."

She bolted out the door as if escaping the plague. Maggie and Ginger exchanged grins as they followed her out.

"Oh my god," Claire said as soon as they met her outside. "Did you see her belly? The whole thing was like granite. I didn't even know the body could do that."

"Which is why I've always maintained that simulated contractions would be all the birth control some women would ever need," Ginger said.

"Birthing is not for the weak," Maggie agreed.

"That would be me," Claire said. "Sheesh, as soon as I see Pete, I am going to kiss him right on the mouth and thank him for not wanting to be a dad."

Maggie felt a spurt of annoyance that Claire had had the smarts to iron that talk out in the very early stages of dating while she, being a dope, had not, and now she had no idea if Sam wanted kids. And truthfully, it was kind of freaking her out.

They resumed their spots in the still-vacant waiting room. Ginger paced for a bit before she settled down. Maggie debated going for coffee but as the time wore on, she didn't want to have caffeine ruin her ability to nap. When two hours had passed, Claire looked like she was about to explode.

"I'm sneaking back there to see what's happening," she declared.

"You can't," Ginger said. "They could be at a critical moment in the birthing. Besides, this time really needs to be just for them."

"But I can't take it anymore," Claire said as she shoved her fingers into her hair. "What if she needs us?"

"Michael would have sent someone to get us," Maggie said. "Joanne's a tough girl from New York. She's going to be just fine."

"What about the baby?" Claire asked. "It's early."

"Not that early," Ginger said. "Just a few weeks, and due dates are always a little fuzzy anyway, especially if you're trying really hard."

Maggie grinned. "It's true."

"Okay, but I'm just going to take a peek to be sure," Claire said.

"Fine," Ginger said in a resigned voice. "I'll go with you."

"I'll hold the fort," Maggie said.

The two friends walked into the maternity ward as if they were expected. Maggie shook her head. It seemed like just yesterday that she and Ginger were here starting their families. Now Laura and Aaron were adults, and days filled with sticky jam kisses and broken crayons were long over.

"How's it going?" a voice asked from the door.

Maggie spun around, and there stood Sam. He was still in his work clothes, but his tie was loose, hanging lower than his unbuttoned collar.

"It's going," she said. She crossed the room and gave him a big hug just because he looked like he needed it. "Ginger and Claire are doing baby recon."

Sam grinned. "So it's not here yet?"

"Not yet," she said. "Did you come by to wait with us?"

"I wish I could," he said. "This is just a check-in. I've got to go back to the office after this."

Maggie studied his face. He looked as if something heavy was on his mind.

"What is it?" she asked. "What have you found out?"

He hesitated as if he didn't want to tell her.

"Oh, come on," Maggie cajoled. "If you told Summer and Blair then it's only a matter of time, likely minutes, before I find out. You know gossip moves at the speed of light in St. Stanley."

He kissed her head and then nodded.

"Okay. While running background checks, I discovered what I suspected, that the lives of Terry Knox and Bruce Cassidy intersected about ten years ago in California."

"So they knew each other?" Maggie asked.

"Yeah, and they were definitely close enough for Knox to kill Cassidy and take his identity," Sam said.

Chapter 23

"How did you . . . oh, my . . . are you sure?" Maggie asked.

"Pretty sure," Sam said. "Terry Knox rented a guest-house from Bruce and Sela Cassidy for about a year, then the Cassidys up and left for Europe, leaving Knox to oversee the estate."

"Well, that seems straightforward enough," she said.

"Yes, except the Cassidys never came back, the house and guesthouse were abandoned and Terry Knox disap-peared. There is literally no record of him after he left the guesthouse."

"So, you think he didn't really disappear, but became Bruce . . ." Maggie's voice trailed off as she tried to put it together.

"About a year after the Cassidys left for Europe, a Bruce Cassidy reappeared in the Boston area. There was no Sela with him. However, former coworkers of Bruce Cassidy—he had no family—received a few postcards from Europe over the years supposedly from Bruce and Sela saying that they loved it there and were never coming back."

"Weird," Maggie said. "So do you think they're really in Europe and this Terry just borrowed their name?"

"No, the financial trail indicates that Terry assumed both Bruce's identity *and* his fortune," Sam said.

"Whoa," Maggie said. "And no one has seen Bruce or Sela since?"

"No," he said.

"Do you think he murdered them both?" Maggie asked.

"I'm afraid so," Sam said. He rubbed a hand over his eyes.

"Is there any way to prove it?" Maggie asked.

"The house was sold a few years ago for back taxes," Sam said. "The San Diego PD is going to search the premises to see if they find any forensic evidence to indicate a crime, but after so much time, I don't know what evidence might be left."

"It seems like Terry must have had an accomplice, though, doesn't it?" Maggie asked. "I mean, how else, if he doesn't have a passport, could he have mailed the postcards?"

"He could have bought someone off on their way to Europe," Sam said. "If he asked someone on their way to Munich to mail a postcard for him, they might have done it, thinking nothing of it."

"I suppose," Maggie said. "But then who murdered Terry Knox? It had to be someone who knew his secret."

"I'm trying to track down whether he had any family or friends in San Diego who might have gotten wise to him," Sam said. "But ten years is a long way to dig."

Maggie thought about the man she had known as Bruce Cassidy. "I have to say, he didn't give off a killer vibe when I met him."

"The scary ones never do," Sam said. Maggie shivered, and he hugged her close. "My theory as of now is that someone knew his secret and that someone killed him because of it. I suspect whoever killed Knox thinks he told Blair about his scam and that's why they're coming after her now—to keep her quiet so they can take the money and run."

"So you think they're doing to him what he did to the Cassidys," she said.

"Yes, but they're a lot sloppier," he said.

"Blair must be terrified," Maggie said.

"I've got a detail assigned to her twenty-four/seven," Sam said. "But not knowing who we're looking for makes it tricky."

The doors to the ward opened and Ginger and Claire came rushing out.

"She's pushing!" Claire cried. "The baby is almost here!"

Maggie glanced at Ginger and saw her brown eyes sparkle with excitement as she confirmed, "Any minute now."

"Whoa! We're having a baby," Sam said. His eyes went wide, and then he threw an arm around Maggie's shoulders and pulled her close. "Isn't this exciting?"

"I have to text Roger," Ginger said. "He wants to be here."

"Pete, too," Claire said. They both scrambled for their phones.

Maggie looked at Sam. "You sure seem excited about this."

"Well, yeah," he said. "I mean, Michael and I are pretty tight since his employee was murdered a few months ago. He still has nightmares about it. I tried to help him, but you know what really got him moving forward?"

Maggie shook her head.

"Knowing he was going to be a dad," he said. "It's been pretty amazing to watch him embrace the life change. He and Joanne are going to be the best parents."

"Yeah, I know," Maggie said. She was touched by how much Sam cared about their friends. It meant a lot to her that Sam had been there for Michael when he needed him, but there was a little part of her that wondered if Sam was excited because he wanted to be a dad, too.

"Roger is on his way," Ginger declared.

"Pete can't get away as there's a band playing at the shop tonight and he's short-staffed, but I am to give him minute-by-minute reports," Claire said.

"When you had Laura, how long did it take?" Sam asked.

"Just a few hours," she said.

"Same here," Ginger said. "And Joanne's been in there a few hours so I'm sure it will be any second."

"I'll bet you were brave," Sam said. His gaze was full of tenderness and Maggie didn't have the heart to disillusion him. How lucky for her that Ginger had no problem with doing so.

"Brave?" Ginger laughed. "She wailed like a banshee. We thought she was dying. Her mom almost called the pastor in to wait with us just in case."

"I was not that bad," Maggie said. "And you should talk. I heard language come out of your lips that I am quite sure your mother would have scrubbed your mouth out for using."

Ginger laughed. "Roger has never let me live that down."

The doors to the maternity ward opened and Michael came out. He looked jubilant, which Maggie took as a sign that all had gone well.

"We did it! Well, Joanne did it. She was amazing," he said. His grin was one of pure joy. "And we now have a healthy, beautiful bouncing baby girl."

"Ah!" Claire and Ginger shrieked together as they hugged each other and then began to cry in a combination of relief and happiness.

Sam hugged Maggie tight and kissed the top of her head. Maggie squeezed him back and then stepped forward to hug Michael.

"Congratulations," she said, feeling her own eyes get watery. "That's wonderful."

"Can we see her?" Claire asked as she and Ginger hugged him and Sam shook his hand.

"Joanne and the baby, both of them?" Ginger asked.

"Yeah, come on back," he said. "Joanne and the baby are all cleaned up and swaddled."

En masse they quietly made their way back to the maternity ward. Gone were the machines and the staff. In the dimly lit room, it was just Joanne propped up in bed with a bundle in her arms.

She glanced up when they entered, and the light in Joanne's eyes made Maggie's throat get tight. Motherhood was all Joanne had ever wanted. To see her holding her baby in her arms after all the years of trying—well, it was pretty awesome.

They all gathered around the bed. Claire and Ginger got the first peek beneath the pink-and-blue-striped flannel. A gauzy little cap covered the baby's head. Her eyes were closed, and the lids had a sheen to them from the goo the nurses put on right after she was born, but her round face was plump and pink and she looked the picture of contentment in her mother's arms.

When Ginger and Claire stepped aside, Sam and Maggie moved in to get a peek.

"She's beautiful," Sam said. "Just perfect."

"She really is," Maggie agreed.

"Do you want to hold her?" Joanne asked.

Maggie eagerly held out her arms, and Joanne carefully handed her the baby.

"I haven't held one this small since my grandnephew," Maggie said. She pressed her cheek to the baby's head. "There is nothing so amazing as a newborn."

Sam smiled at her, and she noted the way his eyes

crinkled in the corners. "You look good with a baby in your arms."

Maggie wondered if he thought they were having a moment, like this could be them. This could not be them. She was not having another baby, and she didn't care how cute the baby daddy was or how much she loved him.

She decided to cut the moment short lest Sam get any crazy ideas. She saw Ginger behind Sam and said, "Here you go. Your turn."

Ginger practically snatched the baby out of her arms. "About time. You were baby hogging," she said.

"I was not," Maggie said. Ginger gave her a look. "I wasn't."

Ginger studied the tiny little face and took a big inhale as if she were smelling a bouquet. "Fresh out of the oven baby smell. I love it."

"So, what are you naming her?" Claire asked. She was peering at the baby over Ginger's shoulder as if trying to determine what would be a good name.

Maggie noted the non-answer and glanced up to see Joanne and Michael staring at each other.

"We don't know yet," Joanne said. "We have a couple of possibilities, but we're going to see which fits best over the next few days."

"*Claire* means *bright and famous*," Claire said. "Just, you know, if you're really stuck."

Joanne and Michael exchanged a smile.

"We'll consider adding it to the options," Michael said. "Right now, we're just happy that mom and baby are a-okay."

"Amen to that," Ginger said.

Sam's phone chimed and he pulled it out of his pocket and checked the screen. "I have to take this. Excuse me."

He gave Maggie's hand a quick squeeze as he walked out the door into the hallway. She watched him go, knowing that this was his life. Always on the job, always on the case—there were no days off for the sheriff of a small town.

"The Cassidy case?" Michael asked as he moved to stand beside her.

"Yeah," Maggie said. "But let's not think about it. You're a dad! How wonderful is that?"

Michael grinned and threw an arm about her. "Pretty darn wonderful!"

They spent some more time cooing over the baby, but when Joanne yawned Maggie took it as a signal to let the new family rest.

"Will you be going home tomorrow?" Maggie asked.

"Yes," Joanne said. "Bright and early."

"I'm bringing dinner tomorrow," Ginger said. "So don't you worry about a thing."

"Oh, you don't have to," Joanne protested.

"I know I don't have to, but I want to," Ginger said.

"And I have the night after that," Maggie said.

"And then me," Claire chimed in.

Joanne snuggled her baby close. "I'm so glad I became a Good Buy Girl. I'll have to raise you up to be one, too."

"She's already in the club," Ginger assured her.

With hugs and kisses and one last glance at the baby, Ginger, Claire and Maggie left the family to their bonding and headed back to the waiting room.

They were just gathering their things and throwing out the empty pizza box, when Sam popped back into the room. "Sorry about that."

"Is everything all right?" Maggie asked.

"Yeah, that was just Blair checking in," he said.

"Checking in?" Ginger asked.

"Every hour, like clockwork, whether I want her to or not," he said. He shrugged. "She's scared."

"Understandable," Maggie said. "If someone shot at me, I'd be skittish, too."

"Can I give anyone a lift home?" Sam asked.

"I have my car," Ginger said. "But I'm sure Maggie could use a lift. Claire, I can drop you off at Pete's on the way."

"Perfect," Claire said. "See you two later."

Ginger and Claire exited the hospital in front of them. Maggie glanced at Sam. "It looks like my ride just ditched me."

"Lucky me," he said. He put his arm around her and together they left the hospital and walked to his patrol car parked just off the main entrance.

"So, you get to just make a parking spot wherever you feel like it?" Maggie teased.

"Perk of the job," he said. He handed her into the front seat and then circled around the car to the driver's side.

"Do you have to head back to the station, or do you have time to grab dinner?" Maggie asked.

This was it, she decided. The aftermath of seeing Joanne and Michael and their baby was the perfect time to ask Sam if he wanted a family of his own, and no matter what his answer was, she would deal with it in a mature and reasonable fashion. And she most definitely wouldn't cry.

"Dinner, definitely," he said. He paused to look at her. "Are you all right?"

"Fine." Maggie gave him a quick nod. "Just emotional."

"Babies will do that." Sam nodded.

As soon as Sam pulled away from the curb, his radio crackled to life.

"Sheriff, we have a call of a two-eleven at a shop on Main Street. Do you read me?" the dispatch officer's voice asked.

"Roger that," Sam said as he clicked a button on his handset. "What's the address?"

"Thirty-nine Main Street," the officer said.

"Thirty-nine? What?" Maggie cried. "That's my address. What's a two-eleven?"

Sam's face was grim. "Burglary."

Chapter 24

"You mean I'm being robbed? Step on it, Sam!"

"On our way," Sam said. He put down the radio and stepped on the gas.

He flashed his lights only twice to move other cars aside, but he didn't use his siren. Maggie wondered if it was to keep from scaring off the burglar. Who would rob her shop? She didn't have anything of extreme value.

Sam parked along the side of the building. "I'm going to check the front first. Stay here."

He was out of the car before she could protest. Maggie stared out the window but she couldn't see around the corner to see what, if anything, had happened to her shop. She tried to wait, really, she did. But this was her livelihood now and she couldn't just sit there while someone ripped her off.

Maggie pushed out of the car and made her way to the corner of the brick building. She only planned to peer around the back to see what was happening—after all, Sam couldn't be in two places at once—but when she saw who was standing in the shadows, rattling the doorknob, she stepped forward.

"Maxwell Button!" she cried. "What are you doing trying to break in to my shop?"

"What do you not understand about 'stay here'?" Sam asked as he came up behind her.

"I stayed," Maggie said. "For a minute."

Sam rolled his eyes. "What if it hadn't been Max?"

"We can't argue about it, because it is Max," Maggie said. She spun back to face him. "Speaking of which, what are you doing here, Max?"

She strode forward, and as she drew near, she noticed Max was wearing a suit. The light went off in her head and she cried, "Tonight! You're proposing to Bianca tonight?"

"Tomorrow, actually. If I could get my ring, I was going to take it over to Doc's to sort of grease the wheels for his approval. I know he and Bianca are new at this father-daughter thing since they only discovered each other a few months ago, but I want to do it right," Max said. "Is the suit too much?"

"No, it's perfect," Sam said. "Doc will approve, don't you worry."

"Why didn't you call me?" Maggie asked.

"I did," Max said. "Like a bazillion times."

"Oh, I shut my phone off in the hospital," Maggie said. She cringed. "I'm sorry, Max."

"Hospital?" Max asked. He looked concerned. "Are you okay?"

"I'm fine. Joanne had her baby," she said. "A baby girl."

"Oh, that's awesome," Max said. "And they're both okay?"

"They're perfect," Maggie said. "But come on, you need your ring."

She retrieved her keys out of her purse and unlocked the back door. Then she led the way to the safe, which was bolted to the floor in the closet. While Max and Sam turned their backs, she opened the safe and took out the velvet box with Max's ring inside. She popped the lid just to make sure the ring was still there. It sparkled at her in all of its flawless glory. She closed and locked the safe and handed the box to Max.

"Good luck," she said. "Not that you're going to need it."

"I don't know," Max said. "It's all about the timing. If Doc approves of my marrying his daughter, then I'm taking her to Richmond for dinner and the symphony tomorrow night. We have balcony seats, and with a little help from the maestro, it should be a proposal she never forgets."

"Oh, Max," Maggie cried. She hugged him hard. "I'm so proud of you. Classical music is her passion—that's perfect."

Max blushed. "Thanks. I took to heart what everyone said. I really do want her to remember this forever. And who knows, maybe, if she says yes, we'll make our two of a kind into a full house, too."

Maggie grinned at him. "That would be amazing."

"Yeah, unless someone beats you to it," Sam said. "Shouldn't you be getting over to Doc's before his porch light goes out?"

Max glanced at the time display on his phone. "Uh-oh, gotta run." He was halfway out the door before he turned around and said, with a wicked grin, "But if that's a dare you're offering, Sheriff, I'm in."

The door slammed shut behind him, and Maggie turned to Sam.

"Explain."

"What?" he asked with a shrug.

"Did you just challenge Max to see who would get married first, or am I hearing things?" she asked.

"Just keeping him motivated," Sam said. "Why?"

As if a dam had burst and caused a flood in a low-lying area, the words Maggie had been chewing on for days came pouring out of her mouth unchecked, unstopped and un-sandbagged.

"Because I don't want to have a baby," Maggie said. "I've already done the midnight feedings, tooth fairy visits, and exploding science projects. If that's what you want, then we have to break up, because I don't want to hold you back. You'll just grow to resent me and you may lose your chance to have the family of your dreams with someone younger who wants the same thing."

Sam stared at her with his mouth agape. He looked like he was about to speak when his phone rang. He checked the display and let out a sigh. He raised one finger to Maggie to indicate he needed a minute. She clenched her hands together in anxiety, not knowing from his expression how he felt about her outpouring of honesty.

Sam barked, "Collins."

Maggie heard a sharp voice on the other end. She could tell it was bad news.

"I'm on my way," Sam said. He ended the call and was already running toward the door. "I'm sorry, Maggie, I have to go."

"Wait, what's happening?" she cried.

"Summer's house is on fire," he said.

"I'm coming with you," she said.

"No, you're not," Sam said.

"Really?" Maggie asked. "You know I'll just follow you."

Sam growled. "Fine, but this time you stay in the car."

Maggie locked the door behind them and they hurried down the sidewalk to Sam's squad car. This time it was an ear-piercing journey with both lights and siren warning anyone and everyone of their impending arrival.

A fire truck was already parked in front of the house when they arrived. From what Maggie could see, they had kicked in the front door. Floodlights on the truck illuminated the house and the smoke that was billowing from the back of it.

An ambulance was parked on the side of the house and Sam started for it at a run. Disregarding the "stay in the car" thing, Maggie was right behind him.

Sam looked over his shoulder and snapped, "Can't you even pretend you're going to listen to me?"

"Sorry, no," she said.

He took her hand in his and they jogged the rest of the way to the ambulance.

An emergency medical technician was working on Deputy Wilson as she sat in the ambulance on a stretcher. Summer and Blair were sitting on the back end of the ambulance, and they both looked pale and disheveled, but not harmed.

"Deputy Wilson, are you all right?"

"Fine." She coughed. She didn't sound fine, and she didn't look fine either.

The EMT was a handsome black man, and he gave Dot a concerned look and said, "She has smoke in her lungs and some second-degree burns. She'll be all right but I want to take her to the hospital."

"She's a hero," Blair Cassidy said. "We were asleep but she woke us up and got us out."

"Any idea what started the fire?" Sam asked.

"Oh yeah," Dot said. "A Molotov cocktail thrown at the house. It exploded on impact. Whoever did it was traveling on foot, and I only know that because I happened to be looking out the back window when they tossed it."

"A drink?" Blair asked. "They threw a drink at the house?"

"A Molotov cocktail is a handmade bomb," Sam said. "A glass bottle full of gasoline with a kerosene-soaked rag in the mouth that serves as a wick. It's used more to light things on fire than blow them up."

"Well, mission accomplished there," Summer said. She was looking at her house with large, sad eyes.

"Who would do such a thing?" Blair asked. "We could have perished in a fiery death."

"Wild guess, but I'm betting it's the same person who shot at you," Dot said. She broke into a coughing fit, and Sam and Maggie exchanged a concerned glance.

"Hospital, Deputy Wilson." Sam said it sternly as if he expected a fight.

"But I need to give a description and I want to canvass the area behind the house," Dot protested. "I know about where I saw the person, and maybe there is some trace evidence left behind."

Sam looked at the EMT for input. He was a good-looking man with broad shoulders, close-cropped brown hair and a kind smile. His badge had a medical symbol on it and the name JAVIER.

"Officer Wilson," Javier said. His serious tone indicated he was about to deliver bad news.

"The name is Dot," she said. She gave him a coquettish smile, which somehow was extra charming with the oxygen tube running under her nose.

"Dot." He said her name with a grin. "As the man who has just tended your burns and put you on oxygen"—he paused to adjust the plastic tubing that ran from her nose and over her ears to the oxygen tank strapped to the wall—"I am asking you to please go to the hospital and not let my hard work be for nothing. It would be a shame if something bad happened to a fine-looking woman such as you."

Dot's eyes went wide. She leaned over to glance around him at the others.

"Is he flirting with me?" she asked Maggie in a whisper loud enough for everyone, including Javier, to hear.

Maggie glanced at the EMT, who was grinning at Dot as if he thought she was about the coolest thing he'd seen all day.

"Yes, I believe he is," she said.

"Well, isn't that something?" Dot asked. "And I'm in uniform and everything."

"I like a woman in uniform," Javier said, and he wiggled his eyebrows at her. "And just so you know, I can't ask you out if you go against medical advice. It would start our relationship off on terrible footing."

Dot gave him an intrigued look and said, "Get a load of you."

"She needs to go to the hospital," Javier said to Sam.

Javier did not look like he was willing to debate the issue, and Sam looked back at Dot with his forbidding sheriff's face.

"Hospital," Sam said to Dot. "I'll protect the scene. If there is anything to see, you can do it in daylight tomorrow."

Dot punched the stretcher in frustration. "Cute EMT or not, tomorrow will be too late. We have to move on this now."

She then broke into a fit of coughing that only served to prove Javier right.

"Medic!" a voice called.

They all turned to see one of the firemen being carried

out of the house. He was holding his arm at an awkward angle. Another EMT waved to Javier from the group of firemen, obviously wanting backup.

"I'll be right back," Javier said. He frowned at Dot. "Do not go anywhere."

Dot gave him a sulky nod and he dashed away to help his colleague with the fireman.

"I'm going to check out the house," Sam said. "Ladies, why don't you all sit in the ambulance with Deputy Wilson and keep her company."

Maggie knew this was code for *Do not let her out of your sight.* Summer and Blair seemed to get it, too, as they nodded and climbed into the back of the ambulance with Maggie. It was an awkward foursome gathered there, with Blair and Summer on the bench across from Dot while Maggie sat on the edge of the stretcher. The three of them had Dot surrounded, and she wasn't going to be able to escape the ambulance no matter how hard she tried.

"He thinks he's so smart," Dot muttered. "Just because he wears the big badge."

"Tell me about it," Maggie said.

Dot began to cough, and Maggie saw Blair and Summer exchange a worried look.

"We owe you our lives," Summer said. She put her hand on Dot's arm. "Please do what Javier and Sam tell you to. St. Stanley needs a woman like you on the force."

It was the nicest thing Maggie had ever heard Summer say. Dot blushed and fidgeted with the oxygen tube in her lap.

"Thanks," Dot said. "I was just doing my job. Someone

is out to kill you, Blair, and I'll be darned if I'm going to let that happen on my watch."

"Thank you," Blair said. She looked faint and Maggie figured Dot's words did not have the soothing effect she had been going for.

"So, Sam told me that he found a link between Terry Knox and Bruce Cassidy," Maggie said. She thought talking about the case might take their minds off the house that was still ablaze behind them.

Blair nodded. Summer let out a shaky breath and forced her gaze away from the house.

"It looks like Terry murdered the Cassidys and assumed their identities," Summer said. "I just can't believe it. I mean, he just didn't seem like a killer."

"I didn't think so either," Maggie said. She and Summer stared at each other. This was the first time Maggie could remember that they had ever been in accord about anything. It was weird.

"I still think Sam should let me help canvass the area. I saw the person who threw the firebomb," Dot said. "They took off into the woods, but they were dragging their left leg like they'd hurt themselves. I know we could catch them if we get everyone out in the woods."

Maggie frowned. "What did you say?"

"We could catch them if we—" Dot said, but Maggie interrupted.

"No, before that."

"They were dragging their left leg," Dot said.

Maggie felt the blood rush out of her face. She turned

to Blair with her eyes wide. "I know who killed your husband. I know who's trying to kill you."

Blair blinked at her. "Who?"

"Sela Cassidy," she said.

She rose to go and tell Sam what she knew, but the back door of the ambulance slammed shut, locking her in.

Chapter 25

"What the—?" Maggie cried. She banged on the door. "Hey, open up!"

The ambulance lurched forward and Maggie was thrown to the floor. Summer and Blair grabbed onto each other and braced themselves against the wall while Dot clung to the handle of the stretcher she was still on.

"What the hell?" she cried. "See if Javier is up there and ask him if he has lost his mind."

A small window looked into the cab of the ambulance. Maggie hauled herself to her knees and crawled to the front. She pressed her face against the window but could only make out the back of the driver's head. It was not Javier. With a knot of gray hair on top of her head, it was clearly a woman.

Maggie rapped on the glass. The woman turned and faced her and Maggie sucked in a breath. The face wasn't disguised by a surgical mask and cap this time, but there was no mistaking her. It was the nurse who was in the hospital the night Blair had been shot. Maggie suspected she was no more a nurse than Maggie was. In fact, Maggie would stake her shop on it. The woman driving the ambulance had to be Sela Cassidy!

Maggie stared at her. Then she rapped on the glass with her knuckles and yelled, "Stop, Sela!"

Sela's eyes narrowed, and then she laughed. The sound was muffled, but even through the glass, Maggie could tell it was unpleasant.

"Hey!" Maggie slapped her palm against the glass. "I said stop!"

Sela ignored her. She gave Maggie a nasty look, then turned back to the front and cut the wheel hard to the right, causing Maggie to slam into the ambulance wall and the others to yelp as they struggled to hang on.

"It's Sela," Maggie said as she scrambled to grab ahold of something to keep from being tossed across the ambulance. "Sela Cassidy is driving the ambulance."

"What?" Dot asked. "How do you know?"

"You told me. Sort of," Maggie said as she grabbed a hand strap.

"What?" Dot looked like she wanted to smack the information out of her.

Maggie hurried to explain. "It all fits. Sam said that Sela was a professional skier until she blew her knee out. So it made sense that she would live in Europe, as she would be familiar with the lifestyle. Switzerland would be a natural fit for her. But do you remember the night Blair was shot? The first nurse who came when Blair called was limping."

Summer and Blair didn't get it, but Dot did. She clapped a hand to her forehead and said, "The person I saw running from the house was limping!"

"It has to be Sela," Maggie said. "And I'm going to take a not-so-wild guess and say she's our shooter as well as our arsonist."

Dot slapped her hip. "Damn it! That cutie EMT gave my gun to Sam when he was examining me. Oh, when I see him again I'm going to shoot him!"

"Focus!" Maggie cried. "We're in deep trouble here."

"It's me. She wants to kill me," Blair said, clutching Summer close. "Maybe I can reason with her."

"Mama, the woman shot you, tried to burn down my house and stole an ambulance. Does she seem reasonable to you?"

The ambulance swerved and they all braced themselves again, then they hit a pothole hard and everyone bounced in their seats as their teeth clacked together with the impact.

"We have to overpower her," Dot said. "It's our only chance."

"Chance? We don't have a chance. She's going to kill us all," Blair said. "She may have been gunning for me, but she's not going to leave any witnesses."

"We're four to one," Dot said. "We can take her."

"With no weapons?" Summer cried. "Oh my god, we're dead. Dead, I tell you."

"Calm down," Maggie said. "Dot's right. We have to try to save ourselves. There has to be something in here that we can use."

They each glanced around the interior of the ambulance. The medical equipment did not inspire any brilliant self-defense strategies.

"This is impossible. What are we going to do?" Blair asked. "Throw bandages and gauze at her?"

"How about this?" Dot asked. She yanked the oxygen tubes off her face and hefted the small tank off the wall and into her lap. "I can bash her on the head with it."

"Yeah, I'm guessing she'll shoot you before you manage to crack her skull," Maggie said.

"I'll sacrifice myself," Blair said.

"What?" Summer cried. "Mama, no!"

"Listen to me, baby girl," Blair said as she grabbed Summer's hands. "You are the most important thing in my life. When she stops the ambulance and opens the back door, I will throw myself on top of her, and the three of you run."

"That's—" Dot began to protest, but Blair held up her hand. "It's me she's after, and I'm willing to sacrifice myself for my girl. You two get her out of here."

"Oh, Mama," Summer sobbed.

Maggie looked at Dot and wondered if she had a lump in her throat like Maggie did. Judging from the sheen in her eyes, she did. It just went to show that even the shallowest of people sometimes had hidden depths.

"I still say I can clobber her," Dot said.

"Please don't risk it," Blair said. "This whole mess is

my fault. If I hadn't married Bruce, or Terry, or whatever his name was, then none of us would be in danger right now."

"It's not your fault, Mama," Summer said. "You loved him. You had no way of knowing that he wasn't who he said he was."

The ambulance started to slow. Maggie glanced out of the window. Sela had driven them out of town and into the middle of a wooded area. Maggie wondered how she planned to kill them all. Surely, she had to realize that she was outnumbered and that even if she did get away with it, the police were bound to figure it out. Not to mention that if she killed Dot, it would be a cop killing, which was very, very bad.

"Let us go, Sela!" Maggie banged on the glass.

Sela turned around and gave her a hard, cold stare. She hit a button on the console and her voice came over a speaker into the back.

"Sorry, but you're collateral damage," she said. She said it as casually as if she were commenting on the weather.

"Why are you doing this?" Maggie asked. "We've done nothing to you."

Sela glanced through the small window past Maggie at Blair. "She stole my identity."

"No, I didn't," Blair protested. "Not on purpose. I didn't know Bruce . . . Terry was a murderer. I never would have married him if I'd known."

"What?" Sela cupped her hand to her ear as if she couldn't hear Blair, but Maggie suspected she was faking.

"I didn't know!" Blair cried. Her voice was a piercing shriek. "I promise you I didn't know."

Sela's face went hard and dark. "I'm the only Mrs. Bruce Cassidy."

"Oh, is that the problem?" Blair asked. "You can totally be the widow. I don't mind at all. You can have all the money. Everything. Just let us go."

Maggie looked at Blair with a frown. Did she really think she was going to be able to negotiate her way out of this? She turned back to Sela. The woman looked like she wanted to slap Blair.

"I'm the widow, because I killed him," Sela said. "Terry was supposed to pose as Bruce and keep sending me money, but he fell for you and my money stopped coming."

"Oh, did you hear that, Mama?" Summer asked. "Bruce . . . er . . . Terry wasn't a murderer. She is."

As the weight of her words had pressed in upon her, Summer went from looking cheered to very alarmed.

"Oh, that's bad, isn't it?" she asked.

"You think?" Maggie asked.

Sela hopped out of the front of the ambulance and slammed the door shut.

"She's killed twice," Dot said. "I don't really think four more bodies are going to faze her much."

Blair moved to stand in front of the back doors. "Stay behind me. I'll try to tackle her."

Maggie and Dot exchanged a glance. Blair weighed about one hundred pounds soaking weight. She couldn't even tackle a chocolate éclair without backup.

Dot hopped off the stretcher. She still clutched the oxygen tank in her hand. Maggie and Summer moved in behind the other two. As far as Maggie was concerned, it was a one-for-all-and-all-for-one sort of moment. Somehow she had never imagined that she'd be side by side with Summer Phillips. It just proved that life was ever the surprise even when facing impending death. Maggie really wished she could see Sam just one more time.

"What is she doing out there?" Summer asked. She grabbed her mother's good hand and squeezed. "If she's going to kill us all, why doesn't she just get it over with?"

The grumbling sound of a truck broke through the silence. There was a squeal of tires and the sound of someone braking hard. Maggie ducked low to peer out the window through the front of the ambulance's cab.

"It's a truck!" she cried. "Someone is here. Oh my god, it's Tyler!"

Summer let out a shriek and she bent down next to Maggie to see. "It is him!"

Both Blair and Dot turned to look out the window, too. Tyler's truck went by, spitting gravel as it whipped past them.

The back door was yanked open and there stood Sela, holding a gun. "Out! All of you! Out!" Dot glanced from the canister in her hand to Sela, but the woman was too quick for her. "Try it and I'll shoot you where you stand."

Dot dropped the oxygen.

Tyler's truck swung back around. Maggie glanced up to see him get Sela in his sights. He stomped on the gas and headed straight for them.

"Is that boy insane?" Blair cried. "He'll kill us all."

"Oh, no, you should see him drive, Mama," Summer breathed. "He's amazing."

Sela looked as if she wasn't sure whether to run or not. Then she took up a shooter's stance and fired off three shots at the truck barreling down upon her.

"Tyler!" Summer shrieked.

Still he kept coming. Sela had no choice but to run around the side of the ambulance to get away. Maggie knew she only had seconds to act. She jumped out of the back of the ambulance, feeling the wind from Tyler's truck push her back against the vehicle as he sped by. She rounded the opposite side from Sela and headed for the driver's side door.

She yanked it open and yelled, "Hang on!"

She turned the key in the ignition and shifted into drive just as she felt the cold metal barrel of a gun being pressed into her left temple.

"Shut the engine off now," Sela said. She was standing just outside the ambulance in the open door Maggie had neglected to shut in her haste to start the engine.

Maggie's hands shook as she reached for the key. The sound of a siren ripped through the night as a patrol car with flashing lights raced toward them.

"You'll never get away," Maggie said. She didn't turn the engine off, hoping the siren would distract Sela enough to give her a chance to put it in drive and hit the gas.

"Sela Cassidy won't, but Blair Cassidy will. Once I kill her and take her identity, I can start all over someplace far away," Sela said. "With my new identity, I'll get all of my money back."

"Don't count on it," a voice said from behind her.

Sela whipped around just in time to take an oxygen tank to the side of the head. She dropped like a stone. Summer stood over her looking ready to hit her again if she so much as batted an eyelash.

Dot was on top of Sela, snatching her gun away and fastening cuffs to her wrists. Both Tyler and Sam had parked their cars and were coming toward them at a run.

Maggie switched off the engine, for good this time. Her knees were knocking so hard she didn't think she could stand, so she let Sam push the door all the way open and grab her.

"Don't ever scare me like that again," he said.

Tyler was squeezing Summer as if he'd never let go. Dot was standing with one foot on Sela.

"Help!" a voice called.

"Oh, Mama!" Summer cried.

They all hurried around the ambulance to find Blair stuck in the back, trying to get down without using the arm that was still in the sling. Tyler reached forward and plucked her down, setting her on her feet.

"You have excellent timing, Mr. Fawkes," Blair said.

He gave her a shy smile. "Please call me Tyler. Since I am going to be marrying your daughter and all, it only seems right."

"What?" Summer asked.

"You heard me," Tyler said. He frowned at Summer. "You love me and you need me and I do not want to hear that you have to think about it or any other nonsense. We were made for each other. That's that, and we're getting married."

"Oh, Tyler." Summer threw herself into his arms, and he kissed her as if his very life depended upon it.

Chapter 26

Sam put his arm around Maggie and pulled her close. "There must be something in the air."

"Post–Valentine's Day insanity," Maggie said. "I'm pretty sure."

"Either that or they're onto something," he said.

Maggie glanced at Sam and saw a glint in his eye that she couldn't interpret.

"Hey, Sheriff, she's coming around," Dot said.

Sam let go of Maggie and strode over to where Sela was lying on the hard ground. He scooped her up and carried her into the back of the ambulance.

"I'll ride with her," he said. "Can you drive?"

Maggie nodded. She glanced down at her hands. They

had stopped shaking, so she was pretty sure she could manage it.

"I am not getting into the back of that vehicle again," Blair said.

"There's no need," Tyler said as he and Summer broke off their passionate clinch. "I'll take you to the station."

"Thank you," Blair said. She hesitated, and then reached forward and patted his arm like she was patting a stray dog that she wasn't quite sure was friendly. Tyler actually blushed.

Blair and Summer climbed into Tyler's truck while Dot climbed into the back of the ambulance with Sam and Sela, who was still a bit loopy, with a growing knot on her head. Sam took a minute to hook Dot up to another oxygen tank as she started coughing and wheezing from the exertion of tying Sela up.

When he gave her the thumbs-up, Maggie closed the doors. She pressed her head against the cold metal for just a moment, grateful that they had survived a situation that could have gone tragically wrong.

After she climbed into the driver's seat and buckled her seat belt, she started the ambulance and pulled out of the woods, turning down the road toward town. She was so relieved that they were alive, she almost turned on the siren, but good sense prevailed and she chose to hum a happy melody instead.

"And then what happened?" Ginger asked.

A day had passed since the fire and the showdown in

the woods. They were all at Michael and Joanne's, who had insisted that everyone come over for dinner so they could hear the story of Maggie and Sam's adventure firsthand.

Michael had brought home a huge deli platter, and the rest of them pitched in with side dishes and dessert.

"Apparently, Tyler heard on his scanner that Summer's house was on fire and he came rushing to the scene, but when he saw that the ambulance was leaving in the opposite direction of the hospital, he got suspicious and called Sam. That's when they gave chase," Maggie said.

"I think I will be in debt to Tyler forever for that one," Sam said.

"After the cavalry arrived, we took Sela and Dot to the hospital to be checked out," Maggie said.

"And when they were given the all clear, Dot went home and Sela was arrested for the murders of Terry Knox and Bruce Cassidy," Sam concluded.

"Incredible," Michael said.

He handed Joanne a plate of food and went to fetch her a beverage.

Maggie had always like Michael, but watching how solicitous he was of Joanne endeared him to her all over again. She remembered how fragile she had felt after Laura was born and how the helping hands of her sister, mother and husband had gotten her though those first few terrifying weeks.

Joanne was sitting on the couch with the baby in the bassinet beside her. When the baby started to fuss, she went to put her food aside, but Sam stepped close and said, "I'll hold the baby for you. You need to eat."

Joanne gave him a weary but grateful smile. Maggie watched as Sam picked up the tiny little bundle and cradled it in his arms. He walked around the room, smiling down at the petite infant, and Maggie felt her heart ache. He would make such an amazing father.

"There's one thing I don't understand," Roger said. He was sitting on the love seat beside Ginger. "How did Sela convince Terry to impersonate Bruce?"

"Yeah," Pete said. He was standing at the kitchen island with Claire while they loaded their plates. "He had to be an accomplice to the real Bruce Cassidy's murder, didn't he?"

"We may never know," Maggie said. "Sela is recanting the confession she made to us right before she tried to kill us. She's saying that the whole thing was really Terry's idea and that he threatened to frame her for her husband's murder if she didn't flee to Europe and mail postcards saying that she and Bruce had moved there and weren't coming back."

"But that story doesn't fit Terry Knox's profile," Sam said. "His personal history is that of an easygoing, odd-job guy who was never in trouble with the law and kept his life fairly simple. We're hoping that some sort of evidence can be found at their old residence to implicate Sela in the murder of Bruce Cassidy."

"Where does this leave Blair Cassidy?" Pete asked. "Was she even really married?"

"No," Sam said. "Bruce used his fake identification for the marriage license, making it null and void."

Maggie and Ginger exchanged a look.

"Does this mean she'll be staying in town?" Ginger asked.

"Last I heard she was looking forward to planning the nuptials for Summer and Tyler," Sam said. "Apparently, Tyler is quite the successful dabbler in the stock market and is much more well-off than Blair imagined. She is now welcoming him into the family with open arms."

The baby stretched and yawned, and a tiny fist popped out of her swaddling. Sam caught it between his thumb and index finger and watched in fascination as her little fingers wrapped around his finger. He glanced up and said, "She's got quite a grip. Have you two picked a name as yet?"

Michael and Joanne exchanged a glance. Maggie could tell it was the nervous look of parents who weren't sure how the name of their baby was going to be received.

Joanne cleared her throat. "Because she took her sweet time in the making and in the arriving, we decided to name her the very thing that she taught us: Patience."

"Oh," Claire cried and clapped her hands together. "That's perfect."

Maggie stood and moved beside Sam to look down at the sleeping infant. With her round cheeks and rosebud mouth, she had certainly been worth the wait.

"She looks like a Patience," she said. "Claire's right. It's perfect."

"Agreed," Ginger said.

Sam glanced up from the baby to Maggie and said, "Isn't she something?"

Maggie felt her heart squeeze hard. She could tell by the look on his face that this was something Sam really wanted. A baby, a family of his own—and he would be so good at it.

"All right, Collins, you need to hand over that baby," Roger said. He stood and held his hands out.

Sam turned his back to his friend as if he were refusing. "Get your own baby."

"Mine won't let me hold them anymore," Roger said. "Teenagers, huh. They think they're too manly for a snuggle."

"Fine," Sam said as he handed the baby over with obvious reluctance.

Roger returned to the couch, where he and Ginger cooed over baby Patience. Pete and Claire, meanwhile, seemed content to keep a safe distance in the kitchen.

Maggie glanced at the couples around them. It was so nice to be together in the Claramotta's snug little house, sharing a potluck dinner, celebrating not only the arrival of the new bundle but also the fact that she and Sam had survived their encounter with a killer.

It was in that moment that Maggie knew what she had to do. It was only fair, and she owed it to Sam to do the right thing.

Chapter 27

Maggie was quiet on the ride home, trying to choose her words carefully. She wanted to say what she was thinking in just the right way so that Sam would understand. As they passed the town green, she noticed that the gazebo was still lit up with the strings of red and white that Sam had surprised her with on Valentine's Day. She took it as a sign.

"Sam, pull over, please," she said.

He glanced at her in surprise but did as she asked.

"What's the matter?" he asked. "Are you not feeling well?"

"No, I'm fine," she said. "Would you walk with me?"

Sam looked past her out the window. When he saw the gazebo, he smiled. It was a grin full of mischief, and it made Maggie's heart rate kick up in response.

"It'd be a pleasure," he said.

He parked the car and hurried around the front to her side. He opened the door and took her hand to help her out. The green was silent this time of night and Maggie watched their breath puff out in the cold night air as they strolled down the path together.

"If you're looking to dance in the gazebo, I don't have any music queued up," Sam said.

"That's okay," Maggie said. "We're going to talk."

"Uh-oh." Sam's steps faltered.

"What's the matter?" Maggie asked.

"When a woman says she wants to talk, it never goes well," Sam said. "Never."

Maggie kept moving forward, but Sam had suddenly become an anchor, holding fast to the concrete and not budging. Maggie tugged on his arm, but he was immovable. She turned back to find him fiddling with his phone.

"What are you doing?" she asked in exasperation.

"Texting the guys for advice," he said.

"Seriously?" she asked.

"I'm scared," he said. He gave her a comically nervous face, and Maggie felt her insides pinch at the thought of life without him.

"Come on," she said. "Be brave."

She looped her arm through his and Sam obliged by putting his phone away and walking with her. She could feel him watching her but she didn't look at him until they were stepping up into the gazebo.

Once they were in the gazebo, Maggie felt as if butterflies

the size of bats were fluttering around inside of her. She knew what she had to say, but how?

Best to just get it done, she figured.

She turned toward Sam and took his hands in hers. As they stood looking at each other, Maggie drank in the face that had come to mean so much to her. She was in love with Sam Collins—of that there was no doubt.

Their story had begun on the elementary school playground in this very town. It had wound its way through their adolescence and into their young adulthood, where Maggie had first learned what being in love meant. Then their story turned on them, causing heartbreak for the both of them. But miraculously, it included second chances and falling in love again. Theirs was a rich story. And now it would change once more.

"Sam, I have to tell you something," Maggie said. She hesitated.

"You can tell me anything," Sam said.

He was looking at her in that encouraging way he had, as if there was nothing she could ever do or say that would make him care any less for her.

She licked her lips, and then words she had no intention of saying came out of her mouth, "About what I said before, you know, when I was freaking out before you got the call about the fire at Summer's house, yeah, well, I changed my mind. If you want a baby, I'll do that . . . with you."

Sam dropped her hands and stepped back. Then he put his right hand over his chest. He looked pale and weak like he was having a heart attack.

"Sam? Sam, are you okay?"

He staggered back a few paces and then slumped onto one of the benches that lined the interior of the gazebo. Maggie hurried to his side. She sat beside him and threw an arm around him to support him.

"Sam, what is it?"

"I just . . . I don't . . . I thought you were going to dump me," he said. "And now you want a baby?"

"No!" she cried. "I don't want a baby. I thought you wanted a baby. I thought I was going to have to cut you loose so you could find someone younger to have a family with, but then I decided that I'd rather do the family thing all over again with you than lose you."

He turned in the seat to face her. He looked at her with such tenderness that Maggie felt her throat close up. "Maggie, I have to tell you, I love babies and I love kids, but I don't want to have any."

"What?" Maggie asked. She sat up. "What do you mean?"

"I mean, I love kids and all, but I have nieces and nephews. And if we had a kid now, I'd be in my sixties when it got out of college," he said. "Maggie, I don't think I have the stamina for that."

"But I thought . . . when I saw you with Patience, you looked so happy," Maggie said. "I thought you wanted kids and a family of your own."

Sam leaned back against the rail and drew her close.

"You and Marshall Dillon are all the family I need," he said. "Except—"

"Except?"

"How do you feel about a dog?" he asked. "I'd really like a dog."

Maggie leaned into him, feeling a sweet sense of relief sweep through her. "I'd love a dog."

"Really?" Sam asked. He sounded as excited as a kid.

Maggie nodded. She knew she was grinning like an idiot, but she was so relieved she could barely stand it.

"I guess there's only one thing left to talk about then," Sam said.

"What's that?" Maggie asked.

Sam rolled out of his seat onto one knee in front of her. "I know this goes against every bit of advice we gave Max, but I can't wait, I have to do it now. Maggie, will you make me the happiest guy in St. Stanley and beyond and marry me?"

There was no hesitation, no second guessing and no doubt. Maggie launched herself into Sam's arms, knocking them both down with the force of her enthusiasm.

"Yes, yes, I'll marry you, Sam Collins."

Sam laughed out loud and then he cupped her face and kissed her. It was a kiss that had been a lifetime in the making. It was a kiss that promised a happily ever after for the boy who teased the redheaded girl he'd had a crush on since preschool and for the redheaded girl who'd lost her heart to that same charmer of a boy in high school.

"Aw, what?" A voice broke the moment like a splash of cold water, and Maggie and Sam scrambled to stand, straightening their clothes as they went.

"This is supposed to be my gazebo tonight," Max

Button complained as he stepped out of the shadows, leading Bianca Madison by the hand.

Sam laughed and threw an arm around Maggie, pulling her close.

"Take a number, boy genius," he said. "This gazebo is taken."

Maggie saw a sparkle on Bianca's hand and she jumped forward and hugged Bianca and then Max.

"You're engaged!" she cried.

Max turned a bright shade of red as he hugged her back. "Yeah, but somehow it didn't feel official unless we came here."

"What are you people doing out here?" another voice called. Maggie looked past Max to see Doc Franklin making his way up the walkway with his wife Alice on his arm. "How's a guy supposed to romance his gal with an audience?"

Alice blushed and swatted his arm. Maggie was so happy to see them together it was all she could do not to whoop with joy. She hurried back to Sam and hugged him instead.

A flash of headlights and the roar of an engine broke through the quiet, and Maggie shielded her eyes against the glare. An oversized pickup truck spun around in front of the gazebo, and suddenly music blared out of its speakers.

"What the heck?" Sam asked, looking every bit the sheriff. Then Tyler Fawkes hopped out of the truck and assisted Summer down from the passenger seat.

Tyler brought Summer over to the gazebo and took in

the rest of the couples at a glance. "Well, look at that, honey, we have us an engagement party."

Summer grinned and stepped into Tyler's arms as he began to twirl her around the gazebo. Sam, Max and Doc looked at each other and shrugged. As Sam opened his arms to Maggie, she noticed that Doc and Max did the same with their dates. It was then that the song in the truck changed, and Maggie glanced up at Sam to see if he remembered it, too.

He grinned down at her and said, "Hey, they're playing our song."

As Harry Connick, Jr., crooned "It Had to Be You," Maggie twirled in his arms, remembering the night they had finally gotten together at the Madison ball just a few months ago. She had thought nothing could be more special than that night, but now that she was going to be Mrs. Sam Collins, and as word of the party in the gazebo spread throughout town and couples like Ginger and Roger and Claire and Pete began to appear and join in the fun, she knew that her happily ever after with Sam had only just begun.

The Good Buy Girls
Top Tips for Baby Thrift

1. Ginger and Maggie both know that a baby only wears
    an outfit long enough to spit up on it before it is out-
    grown. Find a family-friendly resale baby store and save
    a fortune on hardly worn baby clothes. You can resell
    the ones your baby outgrows there, too.

2. Joanne has a plan to save money on jarred baby food and
    feed her baby more healthy food in the process as soon
    as the wee one is ready for solids. She will simply puree
    the same vegetables she cooks for dinner and then freeze
    them in ice cube trays, ready to be warmed up for baby
    at mealtime.

3.   Ginger has invested in cloth diapers for her friend, buying them on sale whenever she can. For the initial investment, the diapers should last until the baby is potty trained, saving the parents a fortune and being better for the environment. Having four boys that she used cloth diapers on, Ginger knows she saved thousands of dollars using cloth.

4.   Claire has started a toybrary at the public library. Instead of buying lots of toys that the baby will get bored with, parents can check out new and different toys at the library when they check out books to read. Fewer toys in the landfills and less money wasted on a toy the baby outgrows as fast as their outfit.

5.   Not knowing what gender the baby was, Joanne bought all gender-neutral baby products. This is a great investment, given that baby number two could be a boy, but also it won't hurt the resale value by turning off people who are looking for a gently used stroller but don't necessarily want a pink and purple girly one for the son they're expecting.

6.   When Maggie was a newly widowed single mother, she had to cut out all of the extras. One of the things she did to save money was make her own baby wipes. She has taught Joanne that soft flannel squares sprayed with a homemade mixture of water, baby oil and baby wash do the trick perfectly and, again, are better for the environment.

From *New York Times* Bestselling Author
Jenn McKinlay

CLOCHE AND DAGGER

**THE FIRST IN THE
BRAND-NEW
HAT SHOP
MYSTERIES**

Not only is Scarlett Parker's love life in the loo—as her British cousin Vivian Tremont would say—it's also gone viral with an embarrassing video. So when Viv suggests Scarlett leave Florida to lay low in London, she hops on the next plane across the pond to work at Viv's ladies' hat shop, Mim's Whims, and forget her troubles.

But a few surprises await Scarlett in London. First, she is met at the airport not by Viv, but by her handsome business manager, Harrison Wentworth. Second, Viv seems to be missing. No one is too concerned about it until one of her posh clients is found dead wearing the cloche hat Viv made for her—and nothing else. Is Scarlett's cousin in trouble? Or is she in hiding?

"A delightful new heroine!"
—Deborah Crombie, *New York Times* bestselling author

jennmckinlay.com
facebook.com/TheCrimeSceneBooks
penguin.com

M1340T0613

Penguin Group (USA) Online

What will you be reading tomorrow?

Patricia Cornwell, Nora Roberts, Catherine Coulter,
Ken Follett, John Sandford, Clive Cussler,
Tom Clancy, Laurell K. Hamilton, Charlaine Harris,
J. R. Ward, W.E.B. Griffin, William Gibson,
Robin Cook, Brian Jacques, Stephen King,
Dean Koontz, Eric Jerome Dickey, Terry McMillan,
Sue Monk Kidd, Amy Tan, Jayne Ann Krentz,
Daniel Silva, Kate Jacobs...

You'll find them all at
penguin.com

*Read excerpts and newsletters,
find tour schedules and reading group guides,
and enter contests.*

Subscribe to Penguin Group (USA) newsletters
and get an exclusive inside look
at exciting new titles and the authors you love
long before everyone else does.

PENGUIN GROUP (USA)
penguin.com